Found in the Storm

Tiffany and
Dameon Gibbs

Found in the Storm

GIBBS PUBLISHING CONGLOMERATE

Thank You

To all our friends and family,
we could not do what we do without your
support. It is because of you that we can find a
way out of the storm.

Dedication

We dedicate this book to all our friends and family who supported us through all the long days and nights to bring this work to life. We truly could not do what we do without your support. It is because of you that we can find a way out of the storm.

To our sons, Kyrie and Kaleb, thank you both for putting up with mommy and daddy's long writing times. Without you both being in our corners, we would not know what to do. Like this book, may you both always find a way out of life's storms.

In a small bedroom in southside Minneapolis, Antonio Hampton sits on the floor staring at the ceiling fan as it expands and contracts. With each sit-up, he watches the blades cut through the air like blades of a helicopter. He concentrates on each blade as they hover and chop overhead, like a miniature helicopter surveying the battlefield of his life below.

His brown face was a mixture of concentration and anger, with a dash of confusion. And with each additional repetition of a sit-up, the sound from the blades' churn seemed to become more mechanical. Antonio pushed himself harder and harder until the sounds of thumping blades began to mingle with that of gunfire and explosions. Even the sweat running down his face and into his eyes was not enough to hinder his momentum. If anything, the sting signaled to his mind that he had stopped moving, giving him more reasons to lift and lower his body.

"Let 'em have it," a man barked.

"Dishonorable discharge," a female finished in unison, as a gavel rang out, ending all voices and sounds.

Antonio collapsed onto his back and gazed at the ceiling fan spinning silently, as it always has. After allowing his mind and breathing to settle, he grabbed his cell phone from the nightstand and pressed the home button to check the time—7:25 pm.

Taking one last inhale to compose himself, he picked himself off the floor and prepared to leave. Only minutes later, he was heading down the steps toward the front door, wearing his winter coat and headphones partially covering his ears.

"Where you off to this time of night?" questioned a woman from behind him just as his hand took hold of the door knob.

Stopping in his tracks, he turned to find his aunt Carolee lounging in the dark across the living room couch.

"Oh, hey, Aunt Lee, didn't see you there," he responded.

"Of course, you wouldn't with those headphones as loud as they are. I hear em' from here, was just dozing off."

"My bad," he laughed. "I'm meeting up with a friend at the Red Door. You want me to bring you anything back," digging through his coat pocket for his keys.

"I'm fine. I already grabbed me something on the way in from work," her silhouette casually lifted up a bottle of wine from the floor; and then returned it back to the floor.

"Long day?"

"You don't know the half of it," she said, relaxing back on the couch.

Antonio sighed and nodded, "Bet, I'll be back," opening the door.

"Ok, be safe, Hun. The neighborhood been rowdy since that shooting round the corner."

"Will do," he answered, hearing a cork popping as he closed the door behind him and locked the dead bolt.

Pulling his headphone fully over his ears, he descended the front steps, passing along the center stone walkway splitting their small grassy front yard which was filled with random yard ornaments and decors. Opening the front gate that was barely hanging on its hinges, Antonio stepped onto the streets of North Minneapolis.

****

The walk to Antonio's destination was uneventful, zoning out on the music, he maneuvered his way through the all too familiar neighborhood. Cutting through multiple housing projects, empty basketball courts, and the occasional dark alley, he made good time, arriving twenty-seven minutes later.

Approaching the bar, several locals stood outside the entrance smoking beneath *The Red Door's* large red and orange neon sign. The Red Door sat halfway along the block and was a hangout for local thugs or the few people simply trying to drink their minds clear after a long day of work. Promptly exchanging fist bumps and nods with those outside he entered the bar.

The Red Door was a mix between a traditional sports bar and a lounge, and once inside, it appeared much larger than its exterior led on. A twelve-foot U-shape bar sat at the heart of the building, with four 32" inch flatscreen televisions hanging above for on lookers. Other large televisions were posted throughout the building, showing the local news, ESPN, and music videos, as rap played softly in the background.

Removing his headphones and hanging them around his neck, Antonio scanned the entire dimly let bar.

There were not too many people at the bar, *"Must be a slow night,"* he thought to himself.

A guy wearing an all-gray sweat suit was having a deep conversation with a woman at the table to his far right. The remaining six people sat at the U-shape bar and were being served by the six-foot tall bartender and owner, who goes by the name "Black." Those not familiar with The Red Door could easily and unfortunately, mistake him for the bar's bouncer if he was not behind the bar. Black had a reputation for having a short temper, and more often than not, when his temper flared, someone was going to find themselves tossed out of the bar and in the gutter. And if they did not respond easily to brute force, the matte black Glock tucked behind the bar always did the trick.

Seeing Antonio come in, Black acknowledges with a quick nod, gesturing him over.

"What up Antonio," Black greeted.

"Ain't nothing Black," he responded, stopping in one of the open spots at the bar, giving Black a fist bump.

"It's been a minute since we seen you up in here," Black said as he continued to make a rum and coke for a costumer.

"I know. Been busy," Antonio said, as Black took the customer their drink and returned.

"Anyways, it's good to see you. What can I get yah bro?"

"I'll take a Blue Moon," looking at a table in the back rear corner and seeing who he was here to visit. "Put it on the tables tab," Antonio ordered, nodding toward the table, as he tapped the bar and stepped away.

"Sure, I'll bring it over in a bit."

"Take it easy Black," he said, while flashing the peace sign and walking towards the rear.

Antonio passed by a few customers sitting at the bar watching an NBA game, the Minnesota Timberwolves versus the Portland Trailblazers. He glanced at the game; Portland was up by twelve with five minutes left in the game. With his attention back focused, he stepped up to the table of his host.

Stephon was an old buddy of his from the military. They first met at Marine boot camp, though Antonio later advanced his career in military aviation and Stephon continued with boots on the ground, the two reminded close through their enlistment.

After taking a sip of beer from his glass, "Look at my nig," Stephon greeted, standing to shake hands, giving Antonio a hug in the process.

"What's up, bro," Antonio greeted in return. "I see you still staying fly," giving Stephon a look over. "You were the pretty boy of the group after all."

"Pretty, nah, that's just how I roll," Stephon said with a smile, pulling back his Gucci jacket to show off his designer jeans and shirt. "Life's been good to me since we last spit words, feel me? Have a seat," he gestured to the seat across from him. Taking a seat, "Man, it's really good to see you. It's been too long."

Black brought over Antonio's drink, sitting it in front of him.

"Thanks, Black," Antonio said, grabbing the glass and drinking slowly, taking a moment to savor its flavor.

"No problem. Let me know if y'all need anything else," Black responded, returning to his post at the bar.

"How long it's been exactly?" Stephon continued.

"At least three years."

"Well, today that shit changes," Stephon said, holding up his glass to toast. "To friendship."

"To Friends, those still here and gone. *Hoo-rah!*" Antonio toasted.

"*Hoo-rah!*" Stephon followed. "Anyway, how are you? How's Aunt Lee?" he asked, staring Antonio in the eyes, as if he knew the answer already.

"I'm good. Aunt Lee, she's hanging in there. Still works at the shelter," Antonio said, sipping from his glass. "You know how she is, nothing can hold her down."

"Yeah, she's one tough lady. I guess that's where you get your stubbornness from, huh? But how are you, fo' real?" Taking a sip, his eyes remaining locked on Antonio.

Antonio followed suit and took a long drink, methodically laying his glass back on the wood table slowly. Then, with a laugh, Antonio said, "Stephon, I know you all too well. What's this really about?"

"Straight to the point," he smiled. "Ok. I know you heard how a few of us started working for some rich suits once we returned from Afghanistan, right?"

"There were rumors, as always. Yet, I don't know what that has to do with me," Antonio said, glancing over his shoulder, slowly scanning the bar. *Something or someone seemed out of place, he thought. Yet, all was the same as it was before.*

"The thing is," Stephon added, getting Antonio's attention once more. "I figured I would extend you an offer. Which would no doubt benefit both of us," leaning forward onto the table with his elbows. "More importantly, for you and Aunt Lee. Look, Antonio, it's a simple job. And a job I would only trust to my truest."

"C'mon Stephon, simple. You and I both know how easy it is to throw that word around," Antonio said, shaking his head. "And you know I don't get down with anything illegal. Have too much on my plate as it is."

"That's the thing. I know how you are, believe me, it's clean," Stephon paused, allowing his words to sink in. "Look, bro, I'm sorry about what they did to you. The old geezers forget how it is and what it's 'bout being on the battlefield. Only thing they care about is getting the next set of documents on their desk signed and out the door. And I don't care what anybody says, you made the best call that day, you hear me?" he asked, sipping his drink. "Hell, I would've made the same call. There was too much bullshit happening that day to have anyone playing shit safe. Besides, they only hit you with the book to keep the press off their asses for fuck'n up."

"What eva' the case, that shit ruined my life!"

"So, punch back at the world, and I'm here to help you. Man, listen, you gave all you had to this country, and look how they repaid you. Now, it's 'bout time you do something for yourself. I got a job for you through a buddy of mine up in Warroad, who could use your skills."

"What kind of job?" Antonio asked, his eyes focused on Stephon's every eye twitch or glance. Knowing the simplest of gestures could reveal if he was telling the truth, and so far, he seemed legit.

"The sort requiring you to fly a small package from point A to point B, and done," Stephon explained, using the salt and pepper shakers in the middle of the table to help emphasize his point. "Straight forward. No questions asked, $100,000 stacks in your pocket. Simple and easy. Solving all your problems," Stephon said, leaning back against the booth, his drink still in hand. "I'll level with you; I need you to take this. I have no one else to lean on."

"Me, the last guy. That's hard to believe, coming from the only guy with endless contacts."

"I know, right? But that shows how desperate I need you."

"I don't know, man," Antonio said, unsure of what to do. "My aunt's been talking to folks at her job, they may have something opening soon. I don't want to miss that call."

"Come on, bro. Working with your aunt? Naw, that's too low. You're a bad ass fighter pilot, not a damn janitor or some shit," Stephon continued loudly, getting the attention of others in the bar. Toning his voice down, "See it this way, you'll be doing me a huge favor, like back in the day. C'mon, how far we go back?"

"Far," Antonio added.

"Damn straight," Stephon said, slapping the table excitedly. "Besides doing me a favor, you can make enough paper to help put you and your aunt in a better position. That's something I'm sure of. When have you ever heard of me doing one of us wrong?" he said, removing his dog tags from beneath his shirt, clasping them as though they were some sacred relic. "When have I? This is for life."

"You always kept your bond."

"How 'bout this, you sleep on it. The bus leaves tomorrow."

After finishing his beer, Stephon slid a ticket across the table, exited the booth, and stood next to Antonio. "The opportunity is there, it's your choice to take it," Stephon smiled, patting Antonio on the shoulder. "It was good to see you, bro. Maybe we'll do this again. Tell Aunt Lee I said hey."

Antonio watched over his shoulder as Stephon walked toward the door. He noticed two guys who were drinking at the bar, suddenly pushed their drinks aside, stood, and escorted Stephon out, followed by the guy and girl who were on the other side of the bar; they fell in line right behind them.

"What's this? Stephon has body guards now," Antonio questioned himself as the door shut behind them. He gave Black a look as if asking *"What was that?"*

Black simply shrugged and continued maintaining his bar.

****

Returning home, Antonio found the house cloaked in darkness, the only illumination coming from the living room television. Taking off his winter coat and headphones, he hung the coat on the banister post, and followed the sound of the familiar game show. When he entered the living room, he saw Aunt Lee lying on the couch, sound asleep, a blanket draping around her feet. From the doorway, he watched in silence as her chest rose and fell with each breath. He shook his head when saw the nearly empty wine bottle next to the couch and the glass tipped over on its side.

Feeling a slight chill in the house, he walked quietly over to her and started pulling the blanket up, when an envelope hidden in its fold's fell to the floor. And for a brief moment, Antonio stared at the bold red letters printed on the mysterious envelope before he finished adjusting the blanket to cover all but her head. He grabbed the enveloped from the floor, and turned down the volume on the television. He walked toward the kitchen, peering back to make sure he had not wakened Aunt Lee.

After pouring himself a cup of water, he took a quick sip, and pulled the letter out of the already open envelope. He his eyes immediately locked on the bold red letters, "***NOTICE OF FORECLOSURE**, payment due now.*" In disbelief, he plopped down on the bench in the kitchen nook, his mind racing as he tried to figure a way out of this mess. He wasn't sure how long he sat there taking in the silence of the house, as though it would somehow help to calm his frantic world.

2

Under the cold gray sky of winter, Antonio Hampton boarded a coach bus with his mind deep in thought. It was not long before the remaining passengers boarded, and the bus was on its way to the next destination. Doing his best to get comfortable in the seat that had seen better days, he began replaying scenes from the last few years of his life in his mind. Like the fields speeding past his window, what he was visualizing was just as barren. No matter what he did to fix the picture, he could not help but feel his last few years had been nothing but an uphill battle. His life was like the scene dashing beyond his window of dawning vistas of frozen fields. Miles upon miles of open fields stretching as far as the eye could see. Only months ago, they were green with corn, potatoes, and snow peas that would be distributed and sold across the country.

Antonio was born and raised in North Minneapolis, where the bricks are red, and the gray concrete was often redder. He never regretted his childhood and greatly appreciated how his parents worked hard to better his life. Unfortunately, that hard work was cut short when he lost both parents just before entering his freshman year of high school, forcing him to finish the rest of his years living with his mom's sister, and graduating alone.

He laughed at the thought of being back in high school, and how he foolishly thought the military was his way out of what he considered a shithole of a place.

Oh boy, was I wrong? Even after giving Uncle Sam nearly fifteen years of my life, I found myself back there. Fucking dishonorable discharge my ass. Anyone would have done the same thing if put in that situation! Well, it's time for me to put that behind me. Right now, my luck is about to change, he thought as he gazed out the window.

He was on the long bus ride heading north from Minneapolis to Warroad, Minnesota. Based on what he found on the internet, it was the sort of place you go to rid yourself of the hustle and bustle, an off-the-grid sort of place. Antonio thought back to when Stephon, a friend from the 30th Brigade, contacted him a few weeks ago, informing him about a job he believed would put Antonio back on his feet. With how things were looking for Antonio right now with no job and Aunt Lee possibly facing an eviction notice, having some money in his pockets meant he no longer had to beg his family for an extra dollar, simply for food or to pay a bill. He chuckled at the thought of needing to borrow money after learning all the skills he had acquired in the service the military.

He had to be honest with himself, at first, he was a little nervous. It had been a while since he flew a bird. But after talking to Stephon, he promised that he would help put everything in place and make arrangements with the client so all would go smoothly. To make things more precise, Stephon promised to handle all the legwork and would put Antonio in direct contact with the client leading up to the day. If there was anyone Antonio believed he could trust, it was Stephon. Entering boot camp together, the two of them remained close even after Antonio went on to become a pilot. Antonio smiled again, *the days when life was simple*.

According to Stephon, here was the deal: arrive the day of and get to the Warroad High School football field where a helicopter would be there for him to pilot. He would wait for the package to be delivered, then fly it to an undisclosed location, drop off the package, ask no questions, depart the location, and get paid $100,000 cash. As simple as that—no people, no drama. Just the way he preferred it.

If anything, he was more concerned about wandering around a backwater town, a place no man of color would dare venture alone. But, he figured if he survived a tour in the Afghan mountains, he could damn sure survive a trip anywhere in his own country.

Looking at his ticket, his arrival time was 12:20 pm, giving him a couple of hours to reach the pickup zone by 4:00 pm. With the sun still high in the sky, he unzipped his backpack, removed a pair of headphones, leaned back in the seat, and closed his eyes. As much as he disliked the idea of being on the bus for several hours, he found solace in music.

3

The winds howled ferociously, swaying the barren trees, as the winter storm battered the small city of Warroad, creating near whiteout conditions. It was during this late hour that Lana Morris found herself walking the aisles of Martha's Groceries. Holding a hand basket, she collected last minute items, before she and her family headed for their family cabin to wait out the storm.

Constructed in the late 60s, Martha's Groceries was built to last. It was a typical brick and mortar, mom and pop store. Just about every item in the store was produced locally, carrying everything from bread to the candy lining shelves near the cash register.

"You find all you need, Lana?" asked a friendly voice from the front of the store.

"I'm managing," she replied, as she continued to meander her way through the store grabbing random items to toss in her basket.

Several minutes later, she approached the cash register where the store's owner, Martha, waited patiently, while checking out the world news section of the local paper. Her husband Edgar stood on a step ladder, methodically organizing the shelves on the wall behind her.

Martha and Edgar's family extended far back in Warroad's history, and though they had not had any children of their own, the city in which they had grown up in became their child.

"I can't believe how long it's been since I've been in here. You've done a good job keeping up the place," Lana said, placing items from her basket on the counter. "Oh, can't forget those," she said, grabbing a pack of Skittles from a nearby box sitting on the counter.

"It has been a long time. Seems like yesterday when you and your sister were running around here asking your parents to buy you candy. And with how the place looks, well when your home and business are one and the same, you kinda have no choice," Martha added with a smile.

"I understand that."

"But I'm not going to complain about it. Besides, it keeps me from having to go out in nasty weather like that," she continued, gesturing to the large store front windows and peering at the snow being carried in the gust of wind, creating a small snow tornado. While looking in awe at this creation, Martha noticed a blue 2012 Honda Pilot parked by the curb in front of the entrance. "Oh, is that your car right outside?"

"Yeah! My family's in the car waiting for me. It's nasty out there, but we'll be at the cabin before the worst of it hits."

"Well, I won't keep you longer than need be," she said, scanning the last item. "That'll be $34.83."

Lana inserted her card into the machine and finalized the payment.

"Thanks again Ms. Martha, it was good to see you again. And you too, Mr. Edgar."

Edgar waved and continued organizing the shelves as Lana walked toward the exit.

"Be careful out there and enjoy time at the cabin. Oh, tell your father we said hello and that we still miss his face at services," Martha ended.

Glancing back, "I sure will. You take care of yourselves as well," Lana said as she opened the door and exited the store.

Outside, she was immediately pelted by cold harsh winds. Without hesitation, she pulled her hood over her head, protecting her face, and ran for the Honda Pilot that ran idle mere feet away. "Ahhh," sighed Lana, feeling the warmth of the heater, as she placed the grocery bags in the car.

Her father, John Morris, sat behind the wheel, while her eighteen-year-old sister, Gabby, sat in the back seat, with her earbuds in, lost in her own world.

"You got all your last-minute items? I doubt we'll be able to leave the cabin for at least a few days," he commented as Lana closed the door shut, closing off the bone chilling breeze.

"Pretty sure I've got everything. By the way, Ms. Martha said—"

"Hope you grabbed my Skittles," Gabby asked, cutting Lana off, her eyes remaining locked on her cell phone.

"Nobody forgot your toothaches," Lana quipped, promptly tossing the pack of Skittles onto Gabby's lap.

"Ouch," Gabby winced as the Skittles landed on her.

After making sure everyone had their seat belts on, John shifted the SUV into drive and slowly pulled away from the curb, heading down Warroad's quiet, empty road.

"I can't see how you eat those things. You know they're not good for you right?"

"Could say the same of you."

"Oh, you—," she said reaching back as best she could to hit her sister.

"Ok, ok. Just joking, geez," Gabby laughed.

"You're lucky we're driving," Lana continued, relenting in her attacks to face forward, looking out the windshield at the snow-covered roads, flurries of white rushing past them.

"I'm glad to see things haven't changed with you two," dad smirked.

"Yeah, she'll always be my little, but annoying sister," Lana added.

"But you know you love me," Gabby teased, causing Lana to roll her eyes.

"I'm glad you're back. It means a lot to your sister," her father said, his eyes bouncing between the road and his daughters.

"What about you?" she asked, glancing at him out the corner of her eyes.

For several seconds there was silence in the SUV, only the slushing of snow beneath their wheels and the faint music coming from Gabby's headphones could be heard.

"I think you know the answer to that."

"You were always a hard egg to crack, Pops," said Lana, before unlocking her phone to check on her social media accounts.

"Who would be crazy enough to be out walking around in this mess?" John wondered, as he peered out the windshield at the dark figure on the corner.

Lifting her head, Lana saw someone wearing a winter coat and carrying a small back pack, standing on the corner as they went past. The person held his phone out in front of him as if trying to get a phone signal. Though the light from the cell phone was on, it was not bright enough to illuminate the person's face, yet Lana could not help but feel the figure was locking eyes with her as they drove by. This made her shrink back into her seat, turning her head, trying to avoid the eyes she couldn't see, but knew were watching her.

"Have to be desperate to be out and about in this. Wouldn't want to be him," he sighed.

Lana remained silent, but was strangely drawn to the individual as their image became smaller and smaller in her side mirror, eventually the individual crossed the road and was out of her sight.

"I agree," Lana whispered softly.

****

After a short ride, then turning down a winding, snow-covered dirt road, the Morris family arrived back at their family cabin.

The three did not hesitate to exit the vehicle and rush in the cabin out of the blistering cold.

"Hey, Pops, I'll put the groceries in the kitchen," Lana said closing the cabin's front door behind her, then walked toward the kitchen.

"That's fine. Put them on the island, I'll start dinner soon," he replied, hanging his coat on the hook behind the door.

Dropping off the groceries in the kitchen, Lana walked into the living room, and grabbed a fleece blanket from a basket. She sat on the floor in front of the crackling fireplace. Alone, she glared at the flames as they bathed the open living room in red-orange hues. Although it's been some years since they were last at the cabin together, it felt like home. But if she did not know herself, she would have believed she was actually happy to be back. Lana focused on the warmth and comfort of her cozy surrounds, listened to the crackle and pop of the fire, and watched the timbers being consumed by flames.

4

As the bus pulled up to the bus station, Antonio looked out the window. He saw that the bus station was nothing more than a roadside gas station, like back in the city. He was half expecting it to be a run-down mom and pop shop, with a man standing outside in dirty overalls waiting to pump customers' gas.

"Too many movies," he muttered to himself.

Stepping off the bus, Antonio shivered at the cold wind that immediately enveloped his body, as the brisk afternoon air blew across his face as the daylight started to give way to a steady snowfall. A chill ran through him as he adjusted his coat. Glancing back at the bus, the driver gave him a look that suggested one thing, "*Good luck*," then he pulled off.

Immediately, Antonio received stares from the customers exiting the bus station's store with various goods in hand, watching him, as if something or someone was out of place. Brushing them off, Antonio adjusted his winter flight coat, tightened his backpack, and prepared for the short hike. Using his cell phone, he entered the high school address. The reception in that area was poor. His phone did not show very many bars. So Antonio raised it in the air, turning in various directions, trying to improve the reception.

Standing at the corner willing his phone to get better reception, the slow engine drone of a lone SUV riding along the empty road grabbed Antonio's attention. And as it slowly passed by, he could feel the eyes of someone locked on him through the frost covered windows, but couldn't make out the shadowy figures inside.

With the brief distraction gone, Antonio looked down at his phone. The directions had finally popped up, indicating the school was a twenty-five-minute walk from his current position. Taking in a deep, cold breath that seemed to burned his lungs, Antonio realized he would have to reach the helicopter sooner rather than later to get out of this brutal cold weather. His phone reported the approaching storm would only worsen in the next few hours. His pickup and delivery of the package would have to be executed flawlessly to dodge the storm. Time was now of the essence.

Hearing the sound of a pounding hammer, Antonio looked across the street and saw a man nailing plywood to the windows of the general store. To his left, he saw a young man and woman walking to their vehicle with bundles of firewood in their arms. Seeing the small city prepare for the storm did not help his mood. He figured living this far north, the folks would be accustomed to such weather unless they understood and knew something he did not. It was unsettling to him. Nonetheless, the people's hurried preparation caused him to put more speed into each step.

Battling against frigid winds that chilled him to the bones and walking through six inches of snow that had quickly accumulated on the ground and numbed his toes, determined to not let this weather deter him, Antonio managed to reach the school before the extraction time. With the snow showing little signs of slowing down, he removed his flashlight from his backpack and made his way behind the school as instructed. At the far end of the field, he found his ride tucked away in the corner beneath a winter camouflage tarp. He was told not to worry about having visitors, as it was the weekend, and all school activities were suspended. This eased some of his worries.

Pulling away the tarp revealed an MD530 Light Utility Helicopter. The MD530 was the perfect flight vehicle for grab-and-go cases. It is small, agile, and can reach top speeds of 175 mph. An inspection of its exterior showed the bird was hardly used, as its black paint gleamed beneath the flashlight.

"Time to make it happen," he mumbled, sliding his hand across the helicopter's cold, steel panels.

After taking a brief moment to admire and inspect the aircraft's exterior, he realized time was ticking away. He made his way into the cockpit, powered on the helicopter, and immediately began his systems check.

The feeling of sitting in the pilot seat and flipping on switches had been hardwired into his brain while serving in the military; everything he did was instinctual. And now, feeling the metals, plastics, and taking in the smell again, showed him how much he missed it all. He truly thought he would never experience it again. Maybe this was the opportunity he was waiting for, that second chance everyone always talks about, but in his life, it never seemed to present itself.

With the engines on, he turned on the helicopter's exterior lights. The storm had gained strength since he had arrived. Having the engine running and the heat on, the once freezing cockpit started to warm up. Sitting by himself, he started to worry if the delivery would be jeopardized.

"Should I call Stephon and have it called off," he thought.

Then he remembered that he had clear instructions, *no calls* to the client or Stephon on the day of the job—strict radio silence. Contact would resume at the pickup location; his job now was to wait. But he hated waiting. Currently, he was hundreds of miles from his home back in the city, sitting in some small country town, in the middle of a blizzard.

"Man, I've been waiting for years! I'm done waiting."

He reached in his pocket and pulled out his cell phone. Looking at his recent contact list, he found Stephon's name. With the phone in hand, he rapidly tapped it with his index finger as he contemplated his next move. Before he could dial the number, a light emerged in the distance, grabbing his attention. Placing the phone back into his pocket, Antonio concentrated on the light that was speeding wildly towards him across the football field's frozen turf.

"What the hell?" he whispered seconds before the black truck came sliding to a halt, a few feet from the helicopter.

"Ain't nobody mention this," Antonio muttered, reaching for his black-bladed boot knife, not exactly sure what he was preparing for.

Two figures emerged from the vehicle carrying duffel bags and brandishing assault rifles, their faces hidden by ski masks. Tossing the bags across their shoulders, they headed for the helicopter. As they approached, Antonio gripped the knife handle a little tighter, being sure to keep the weapon concealed at his side.

The helicopter door burst open, cold air and snow rushed in as the two men tossed in their bags, climbing in afterward.

"What the hell are you waiting on? Get the hell out of here," said one of the masked men as he slammed the door shut behind him.

"I'm not sure I know what's going on here. I think there's been a misunderstanding," Antonio said, looking over his shoulder at the two figures, doing his best to keep his composure.

"You're Antonio, right?" asked the smallest of the two figures. Removing his mask, it revealed the face of a well-groomed young man, who looked no older than twenty-five.

Furrowing his brow at the question, Antonio replied, "Yes, I am, but who are you?"

"Well then, I'm paying you to do one damn thing, and that's fly. Not to ask questions," he yelled.

"Fuck this. If he can't understand you, maybe he'll understand this," the other person chimed in, shouldering his rifle and aiming it at Antonio.

Yeah, he's about that life, Antonio thought, his muscles tensing as he prepared himself for anything.

"Put that shit down!" the young guy snapped, pushing the man's rifle barrel down. "It's not like your trigger-happy ass can fly the helicopter. So, relax." He turned to Antonio, "You're not going to get that $100,000 by sitting here. So, I suggest you get this bird air-born, pronto."

Antonio faced forward. Taking a few deep breaths, he quietly sheathed his blade and turned on the engine. *Stephon, what in the hell did you get me into?* The rotor blades came to life, kicking up a whirlwind of snow around the helicopter.

"I knew that would get you moving," the young man quipped to Antonio. "Time for some fireworks!" he continued, moving toward the side door as if expecting to see something in the whiteout. "Blow it!"

Not even a second later, the masked figure pressed down on the remote trigger to detonate the thermite in their vehicle. Suddenly, a fiery ball erupted along with a loud, ear-piercing explosion, destroying any trace of their presence.

Antonio jerked around to witness the chaos behind them. *What the hell? I thought this was supposed to be a quiet operation where we wouldn't draw attention to ourselves.*

"Uh, that felt good," the unknown man mumbled.

The younger man made his way back to Antonio, patting him on the shoulder, and asked, "How soon can we be at the delivery point?"

"No telling with this weather. If there were clear skies, I calculate an hour or so. However, with this storm, it could probably double that." he responded, as the craft became airborne.

"You cut that time in half, and it's another fifty grand for you, friend. No questions asked."

"I'll see what I can do."

"Be sure you know that's coming from your cut," said the other man, his face still hidden by the mask.

"With all the money we just got, it's not going to matter what end it comes from. We're all going to walk away from this richer and more respected men than we are today," the young man replied, pulling on the zipper of his duffel bag, exposing the bundles of cash inside. A big grin spread across his face, making him look even younger.

"Is that money?" Antonio asked, glancing back and seeing the contents of the bag. "Where the fuck you get all that?" *Shit! I knew this was too good to be true, he thought.*

"Hey, no worries, pal. Just know your days of hardship are over. Yes, and you don't have to look at me that way. I know all my clients. Why do you think I had Stephon recruit you? The military or the government may not have use for you, but people like me do. Ain't that right, Lester?"

"Why the fuck are you saying my name?" Lester snapped, eyeing Antonio as he shifted his position.

"No worries, you're rich now!" His words appeared to have calmed the beast as Lester sat back in his seat, not saying another word.

Antonio knew nothing about either of these men, yet the words he spoke were true. Antonio had given everything he had to this country, and what did he receive in return? Nothing. No check, not even a simple loan for putting his life on the line. Instead, he received a dishonorable discharge, which pretty much ruined his chance of ever living a normal life. That dishonorable discharge stood in the way of his present and future opportunities. All he owned was wrapped up in his day-to-day living. Yet this one job, and more like it, could change it all.

"You sure he's ready for this type of work?" the other guy asked in a rough whisper.

"Oh, he's ready. If not, this much money makes you ready. Besides, if all falls through, that's why you're here."

The young man's words were cut short as he was jolted to the side. "What's happening up there?" he asked from the rear.

"The weather, that's what's happening. The conditions aren't good," Antonio said, grimacing as he strained to keep the helicopter level. "Not certain if we should push for the landing zone tonight, visibility is dropping with increasing winds,"

"I hate to say it, but you have no other choice. With this much cash missing, it's going to be too hot for any of us to stick around in the area. The landing zone is the only place this bird is going to settle down tonight. So, make it happen."

Antonio remained silent as he concentrated on the turbulence that began battering the aircraft. These were whiteout conditions. He had been in similar situations before, the difference from then to now was honor. Serving was about honor and dying for one's country. This felt and was different; this was all about money. Was he ready to die for it? Was an additional $100K worth dying for?

Before his mind could choose between the two, the cockpit alarm pierced their ears as a red overhead light kicked on. The aircraft shook violently beneath them. Even with the proper adjustment, the helicopter struggled to stay on course. Strong winds slammed into the hull, forcing it into a spiral. The men's eyes bulged in fear, as they quickly grabbed a hold of their seat with one hand and the bar overhead with the other.

For the next thirty seconds, no one said a word. Their eyes stunned with fear as they held their breath. Time seemed to slow down and the main rotor blades sputtered, then stopped. Antonio felt his stomach drop and then bungee back into his throat. His adrenaline spiked as he gripped the joystick and fought against the wind drafts to try and guide the helicopter down as it fell from the sky.

"Get your seat belts fastened! Now!" Antonio ordered. This is what he had trained for.

Under the flashing dome light, Antonio watched the two men as they frantically struggled to get their safety belts locked while the helicopter continued to spin out of control, plunging them into the darkness below.

Time was running out! Antonio gazed out the windshield at the approaching black abyss below, as it slowly engulfed more of his view. Everyone did their best to hold onto their seats and their sanity, as they fell quickly to the earth below. Their yells echoed through the cockpit, right before impact. Then silence, nothing!

5

The world outside Antonio's AH-1Z Viper flight cabin was like gazing into a black void. The mountains were a dark backdrop, rising like spikes in the distance, just a shade or two blacker than the horizon. There didn't seem to be a star in the sky, while smoke from fires obscured the moon. The soot mingling with the limited moisture in the air did not help the situation. Vehicles and other debris glowed with orange embers within the abyss below.

Antonio's flight helmet, dubbed "The Owl," fed him a binocular display with a 40° field of vision of the battlefield. At first glance, it appeared to be an oversize three-dimensional headset with a large ocular visor. However, the Owl brought everything in darkness into the light, illuminating what the natural eye cannot. Scanning and examining the world below, burning buildings in the distance caught his attention. At a glance, he could tell they were once beautiful works of architecture, but now they were the casualty of the previous battle and were like giant flares in his helmet's display system.

"Platoon Leader, I have you on radar. I see you approaching one click south of Hell's Pass. All is clear," Antonio says as he passes the helicopter high over the battalion of troops below.

Antonio replayed his orders in his head. *He was to provide overwatch for the Thirtieth Battalion as they cleared out the local village and eliminated enemy personnel in the mountain pass.*

"Let's hope it stays that way. You saw how things went yesterday in the battle at Dahaneh. One moment it's beautiful; the next, we're crawling on our bellies," responded a gravelly voice through his ear set.

"It's dark out here, so make sure you keep it clear for us grunts."

"Don't I always?" he replied, scanning the infrared screen, seeing the troops maneuvering along the base of the mountainside, preparing to enter the pass when he suddenly spots movement. "Hold on, 304, I see movement to your southeast, half a click. I'll swing the bird around for a better look."

"Ok, Overwatch. Staying put for now. We'll wait for your call."

"Copy that, 304."

Maneuvering the AH-1Z Viper into position and cloaked by the night sky, Antonio hovered over a two-story structure. It was not long before several people poured out of the building wielding weapons. Against the darkness of the desert, they lit up like Fireflies with infrared glasses. Their trajectory was No Man's Pass.

****

Antonio shook his head, trying to bring his mind back to his current situation. His eyes cracked open wide as he did his best to shake off the lingering vertigo. It took several seconds for his vision to come into focus. With the world turned on its side, Antonio's eyes became big as saucers as he suddenly threw his head to the side, trying to dodge a four-foot branch that came smashing through the windshield and barely missed his head by inches. The howling wind rolled in like a freight train through the gaping hole.

Even though Antonio's body ached from his head to his toes, he smiled, realizing he was not dead, at least, not yet. But he knew he was far from being out of the woods. Uncertain how long he had been out, he figured it had to be for some time. All of the power in the cockpit had been lost. Only the red emergency light flickered above his head, adding the sense of dread to an already screwed-up scenario. Moving slowly, he searched for his bag, which he had placed at his side. A sharp pain shot through his side, causing him to grimace. He immediately leaned back in his seat, taking deep breaths to gather himself and manage the pain.

"You alright back there?" he asked, receiving only silence in return. "Hey, you back there?" Taking whatever strength he could muster, he leaned back, unfastened his safety belt, and braced himself for the fall.

The fall from the pilot's seat was only a few inches, but it could have been several feet with how much pain it caused him on impact. For a few seconds, he laid there clutching his ribs. Orienting himself upright, pain shot through his side. It was as close to what Antonio imagined it felt like to be punched in the ribs by Mike Tyson, bare-knuckle style. With the helicopter on its side, he was going to have to climb over and out of the passenger side, a challenge he was not looking forward to. Before clambering out, he made sure to scan the inside for anything useful when he stumbled upon a black boot. Following it, he traced it back to the rear where it belonged to the young man who had hired him. His skin was now as pale as the snow that blew into the helicopter. There was no need to check for a pulse; the man's head was twisted in an unnatural position.

Most people would panic, and Antonio would have done the same if not for his training. He had never seen a dead body this close before, but he had gone through multiple protocols in case he experienced a crash landing. The first protocol, check for injuries. That was an easy one; he definitely had some. Second protocol, remain calm. Third protocol, get your bearings.

Unfortunately, this was not his first brush with death. He did not even know this guy's name, but he knew someone would eventually find the body. For now, he knew he had to keep moving. The pain in his side throbbed almost on cue and, as he grimaced with each interval of pain, brought the scene into focus. There was no sign of the other man. All that remained was one body and a single duffel bag. Hobbling over, he looked inside the duffel bag to find it filled to the brim with money.

It was at that moment Antonio had two choices, either leave everything and go find help or take the bag and forget this all happened. His mind immediately went back to the guy whose name he did not even know. And for a moment, he thought to himself, *"Should I leave or grab the body?"* Suddenly a gust of cold air slammed against him. "He'll only slow me down," Antonio assured himself.

There was no telling where the other guy landed in the crash zone, and in this weather, it could take days to find him. If Antonio went for help, he risked jail time. What would he tell the police? What had these guys done to get this money? He had not traveled all this way to crash and go to jail for who knows what.

Doing his best to push those thoughts aside, he began to search the body. Finding a flashlight, he used it to locate his backpack and promptly slung it across his back. With another heave, the remaining bag of money was tossed from the helicopter. Finally came the third protocol, "get your bearings," which for him meant climbing out of this forsaken chopper. Seconds later, he climbed from the cockpit, collapsing onto the snow-covered ground.

Lying on his back, he recouped his strength for the journey before him. It was at that moment that he felt a sense of peace as he watched the snow descend from the heavens and blow through the dense trees. *"How can there be peace in the world when there is no peace in the world? Is this what fate has dealt me? To freeze to death in these woods?"* he wondered.

"Fuck fate!" Standing to his feet, he scanned the wreckage one last time. Besides being flipped on its side and having a tree jammed through the windshield, the entire tail end of the helicopter had been torn off. The once pristine bird was now only a shadow of its former self, and he was lucky to be walking away from it.

Removing a small compass he kept in his bag, he figured he should walk southeast, which led back to the bus station. With his duffel bag in hand and clutching his side, he limped away from the crash site, leaving it to become a secret of the dark, silent woods.

6

What seemed like hours passed since he had abandoned the crash site and Antonio continued trudging through the dense wood with no end in sight. Pressing on, he broke off a large branch from a tree, using it to stabilize his walking and combat the snow. High winds beat upon his weakened body. *When did I last eat?* He wondered, as his stomach growled with hunger and his body ached. Taking a quick breath, he leaned on a tree to keep himself upright. His feet felt heavier with each step. Although the walk through the deep snow was exhausting, it was the steady sound of, *crunch, crunch,* beneath his boots which helped to keep his senses alive.

The pain, hunger, and cold were beginning to take its toll as he began to feel himself slipping under the eerie silence of the night. He wondered if he were to die out here, was it worth it? Did his life mean anything to anyone? Hell, would he even be missed?

Tripping on an object, he fell to the frozen earth with a painful thud. His weakened body told him to lay there and rest. But through it all, he resisted the urge, knowing well if he rested his heavy eyelids, he may very well rest them permanently.

"Come on! Get your lazy ass up soldier! I know you don't want to die out here." He muttered, slowly rolling himself onto his side, then on to one knee. "You can do it, you can do…" He stopped short, taking heavy but steady breaths. He spotted something in the distance before it vanished.

He zeroed in on a section of the forest just ahead, hoping to see the anomaly again through the dense trees. As if fate was giving him a second chance at life, the small glow reappeared in the darkness, immediately becoming his beacon of hope. Mustering whatever strength, he had left, he stood to his feet and stumbled toward the light.

7

In their family cabin, Lana fueled the flame by tossing in additional logs her father had recently cut. The fire slowly intensified until its orange flames completely lit up the room. She put the fireplace safety guard in place. Feeling the warmth of the fire, she wrapped her blanket snuggly around her and stared into the flames, as she watched the embers floating above the logs.

She had promised her younger sister, Gabby, she would join them on the next family trip to the cabin and bring in the New Year as a family. It was as if she was a kid again, sitting in front of the very fireplace her great grandfather had built generations ago. Big game trophies decorated the deep, gray stone column that reached the two-story ceiling above. Looking up, the exposed beams of mahogany latticed the ceiling. The fireplace had acted as the cabin's heart for as long as she could remember.

Still beautiful, she thought, smiling with joy.

So much of her life had changed since those days, and this was the first time she had stepped foot into the cabin since leaving for college, a decade ago. Being here had caused a barrage of memories to flood back to her, memories she had buried with the grind of daily life.

She lowered her body to the floor and positioned herself comfortably before the fire. Crossing her long legs, and tucking her hands behind her head, she let out a content sigh, as she stared at the joists and beams making up the intricate roofing. The dancing flames pulled her deeper into memories of her family, as she began to feel a comfort she had not felt in years.

Oh, the stories, she thought when an unexpected knock came to the front door.

"I got it, Pops!" She yelled, hopping to her feet.

In seconds she reached the door and had it open. "Good evening, Officer Blake," She greeted surprisingly.

"Hey there Lana. I didn't expect to see you here this year. It's been a long time, at least seven years," she said.

"Ten to be exact," Lana said, with a smile.

"Wow, how time flies. Well, I have to say you grew up to be a beautiful woman. I know your mom would be proud of that," she ended, a brief silence taking hold of them.

"I'm sorry. Come on in," Lana said, waving the officer inside and out of the snow. "How may I help you?" Closing the door behind her.

"Who is it Lana?" Asked John Morris from the kitchen.

"It's Officer Blake!"

Ambling out to the foyer, "Yoon, how are you?" he greeted her, drying off his hands with a towel, "What brings you this way?"

Officer Blake smiled warmly, showing off her perfectly straight, white teeth.

Gabby descended the stairs, waving hello to the officer, as she joined the small gathering in the foyer.

Officer Blake removed her State Trooper Campaign hat, revealing beautiful salt and pepper hair, which was swept across her forehead and pulled into a neat bun in the back. Her olive skin flushed slightly as she replied. "I'm doing great, thanks for asking. Sorry for disturbing everyone at this hour, but I heard that you were up at the cabin. I came to make sure all was well before the worst of this storm hits, you know, for old time's sake. Once it starts, I doubt the roads will be clear for a few days. It's best if you have all you need before then."

"I appreciate it. But I think we have all we need to ride it out for a few weeks, if need be," John assured her.

"Good to know. Maybe I should trudge over the hill to make sure I don't run out of supplies." She said with a wink.

John cleared his throat, "Well I just finished up dinner, would you like to stay?" He gestured towards the kitchen, "I made pot roast and cornbread."

"It smells amazing, thanks, but I had better get going. I have to check on Ms. Copeland before ten o'clock. We all know how she is about being on time."

"I understand. Once again, we appreciate you checking on us."

"Anytime. Enjoy the rest of your evening and be safe out here." Officer Blake replied, putting on the wide-brimmed hat and venturing back out into the falling snow.

"That was nice of her," Lana said, closing the door.

"She happens to be a good friend of the family," John added, a slight flush coming to his brown skin, before heading back towards the kitchen.

"Friend of the family? More like she wants to be a *really* good friend of yours, Pops," Gabby said, she and Lana both erupted in laughter.

"Good one, Gabby."

"I'm glad you two are finding some amusement on this trip."

"Come on, Pops, you didn't see how she was looking at you? She's a widow, you're a widower..."

"I don't have time for y'all's foolishness. Come on and eat. Dinner is ready," John said, disappearing into the kitchen.

"Leave your father alone," Lana continued, wrapping her arm around her sister's shoulder. "You know he's still getting over mom."

"He's not the only one getting over it. But look at us, we're not letting it hold us back." Gabby said looking into her sister's brown eyes.

Gabby looked like a miniature image of her older sister. Both with big, almond-shaped eyes like their mother, and full lips to match. At sixteen, Gabby was petite and could pass for slightly younger. Their mother had barely hit five feet four inches, and there was no doubt Gabby took on her mother's height, whereas Lana got her height from their father. Both Lana and Gabby inherited their rich brown skin from John.

"True, but let's take it easy on the old guy while we are here. He needs this time. Alright?"

"Whatever you say," Gabby replied, rolling her eyes playfully.

"Now let's go dig into this pot roast! Smells great."

"Lead the way, I'm starving."

****

In the kitchen the three of them sat around the log table, all with empty plates before them.

"Oh my goodness, Pops, that was delicious," Lana leaned back in her chair, rubbing her now stuffed belly. "I haven't had pot roast in a long time. And that cornbread was everything!"

"I'm glad you enjoyed it. I figured I'd give you a nice home-cooked meal after being gone so long. And I can't trust them New Yorkers to treat my baby girl right." he said standing to his feet to collect the dishes.

"Oh, let me get those, Pops; it's the least I can do," Lana replied quickly, standing to her feet.

"No, you don't. You sit down and relax. Don't start trying to treat me like an old man just yet." he smiled and continued to stack the plates to take to the sink. Lana raised both hands in surrender and returned to her chair.

"I'm not sure about you guys, but that meal put me in the mood to do something fun," Gabby chimed in.

"Gabby, most people want to relax after eating a meal like that," Lana commented.

"Good thing I'm not most people." she quipped resting her chin on her palm.

"Sure not."

"What is that supposed to mean?"

"Nothing." Lana smiled mischievously at her sister.

"Anyway, what are we going to do, Dad? It's not like we're going anywhere soon." Gabby asked, as he returned to the table to collect the rest of the dishes.

"How about we watch a movie?" Lana suggested.

"We can watch a movie any night. We need to do something special, something that we haven't done in a while," Gabby said, tapping her chin thinking. "Oh, we can play Scrabble!" she continued excitedly, stopping her father in his tracks.

Surprised at her choice, Lana glared at Gabby, tilting her head slightly.

"What? What did I say?

"That was mom's favorite game," Lana answered, and promptly looked at Pops, who stood at the table silently.

"I'm sorry, Dad. I didn't mean to," Gabby said quietly, her brown eyes beginning to well up with tears.

Instinctively, Lana reached for her sister, pulling her close to comfort her. A nerve had been stricken with all of them.

John inhaled deeply, "Don't worry, sweetie, it's not your fault." He said, forcing a smile, "We can do whatever you…" before he could finish there was a bang at the door.

A few seconds had passed as the three of them remained silent beside the table, then came the second round of heavy knocks.

"I'll get it." breaking the odd silence, Lana stood and made her way to the front door.

It killed her to see her father in this state, she had long realized he had not been the same since her mother, Gloria's death. And she hoped and prayed by being home, her presence could bring him some sort of comfort. She convinced herself this trip would do him some good.

Thump, Thump!

"Alright, I'm coming," she called, jogging the last few steps to the door.

Twisting the knob, Lana opened the door and a body fell with a hard thump at her feet. A high-pitched yelp escaped from her lungs, as she jumped back. Standing over the body, Lana did a quick examination while the person lay face down on the floor. Her first glance revealed it was a male wearing an aviator coat, a large duffel bag at his feet. She remained still while wind and snow blew into the doorway, creating a light layer at her feet. Building up what courage she had, she cautiously knelt to roll him over. With him now on his back, she was able to get a good look at his face through the frozen blood and frost-covered beard.

"What is it Lana?" John screamed from the kitchen, worry peeking in his voice. He shuffled to the door as fast as his arthritic knees would let him.

Before Lana could answer, the man reached up and grabbed her arm, causing Lana to fall back and scream.

"It wasn't my fault," he mumbled, then releasing her arm and passed out.

Keeping her eyes on the man, Lana was frozen with shock, as Gabby and her dad came to her side. "Pops, what do we do now?"

8

Resting comfortably in the AH-1Z Viper, Antonio allowed the helicopter to do what it was designed to do, and that was to remain anonymous. Like a phantom, he hovered the aircraft above the unexpected combatants.

"Come in, 304 Platoon Leader, I have several bogies approaching your position from the southeast, their ETA is twelve minutes."

"How many and are they hostile?"

Looking at the helicopter's monitor targeting screen, he counted the green blips moving rapidly toward the mountain.

"I say close to twenty. And with them waiting till your backs were against the mountains, I wouldn't count on them to be friendlies!"

"Shit! They can't give up, can they? Hold on, Overwatch." the leader ordered, then patched himself to his second in command, positioning himself to glance down at his line of soldiers, "Get the platoon ready, we have unknowns approaching from the southeast. Their ETA is twelve minutes."

"On it!" came back through his headset.

"Overwatch, you still with me?"

"Still here, 304. What's the assessment?" Antonio responded as he hovered silently over the figures, being sure to keep them within his crosshairs.

"Overwatch, we're going to need your assistance on this one. With the hostile mountain pass to our backside and

little to no cover, it won't be good." The leader looked toward the mountains, the peaks appeared threatening, like jagged teeth against the dark of night.

"I got you Platoon Leader. That's why I'm here, to be your guardian angel. Notify your team the Heavens are about to open up," Antonio ordered, making adjustments to the weapons system.

"Copy that, Overwatch!" There was a brief, yet tense silence that came over the already quiet atmosphere when the platoon leader came back over his headset, "Let 'em have it!"

With those words and the boogies already on target, Antonio took in a single breath and latched down onto the trigger. The helicopter was outfitted with Hydra 70 unguided rockets, the aircrafts best systems for air-to-ground combat. In the blink of an eye, a volley of Hydra rockets were streaming towards his mark, the target erupted into a billowing cloud of fire, smoke, and debris.

****

Antonio lurched up from his dream, panting, as sweat beaded on his forehead. Collapsing back down on the bed, he blinked until his vision came back into focus. It took several seconds for him to shake the grogginess. A small candle sat on the nightstand beside his bed, giving the room a yellowish glow. Though he had been out of the military for some time, it had been engrained into his being, to the point it had become instinct to always scan a room for details when entering, never knew with things like the number of exits and

48

people became crucial to survival. Scanning the room, the light revealed nothing out of the ordinary, a rocking chair positioned neatly in the corner, a couple of stacked boxes, and various memorabilia hanging across the logged walls.

Attempting to sit up once again, he grimaced under the pain. It was an indication his body had taken a real beating in the crash. *How long have I been out*? He asked himself, failing to get an idea of the time of day due to the thick curtains which covered the windows. He went to brace himself on the headboard, when he noticed the handcuffs that secured him to it. Antonio looked for something to free himself, and finding no option, he resulted in pulling at the sturdy beam. Then he remembered something, reaching for his boot.

"Looking for this?" a voice boomed from the shadows of the bedroom's doorway. The tip of his black bladed knife flickering in the light. "Don't worry you might get it back later," the voice said, sheathing the blade.

"Where am I, and why am I cuffed to this headboard?" Antonio asked, speaking in the direction of the voice, while raising his cuffed hand.

"You're handcuffed because you showed up at my door, covered in blood, carrying a bag full of money. And there are only two reasons I can think of for this sort of scenario. Either you were going from house to house donating money to families when you were attacked by wolves, or you did something very illegal," the man continued before slowly stepping into the light wielding a short stock double shotgun.

Even in the poorly lit room, Antonio was able to make out the figure wearing a red and blue flannel jacket. He was a man up in age, most likely in his early 60s with a fully gray, five o'clock shadow. Even with his age, he appeared fit and most likely knew how to handle himself in his younger years.

"Which one you going with," Antonio asked, slowly leaning back onto the bed.

With the weapon still aimed at Antonio's chest, "I'm still trying to work out the details of it all. I was trying to figure out why wolves would hurt an innocent man helping out families during a winter storm? But no matter how I spun it, I couldn't work out the details, which leaves me only with the latter," John said, closing the door behind him, then lowering himself down into a rocking chair in the corner where the light barely illuminated his features.

"I see you have it all figured out old man," Antonio replied with a sarcastic slow clap. He winced in pain as he shifted to sit on the side of the bed. "What? You plan to turn me and the money in. Then become the hero of the day?"

"You got that right." John shot back.

"And where's the bag?"

"The money's safely put away. But that should be the least of your worries," John sneered.

"Well, I guess it's going to be some time before that happens, being that I've been out for who knows how long and didn't wake up in a cell. That tells me this storm not only has us trapped in this cabin but has knocked out communication," he smirked. "So let's make this easy for the both of us, you let me go from these cuffs, give me my bag, and I walk out your door as if none of this happened.

And we all go our separate ways, no further incidents needed."

"You should be ashamed disrespecting our country this way. What, let me guess? You let some hard times get you down and you turn to crime? Typical!" John sputtered with disgust "I expect more from an Army man, right Antonio?"

"How do you know my name?"

"I know all I need to know son, better yet, Captain Antonio Hampton," John replied, digging into his inner jacket pocket and pulling out a set of dog tags.

Antonio patted his neck frantically, finding nothing there. "Give'em back!" he screamed, reaching out his hand.

"Why should I? It's not like you respect what they stand for," John continued calmly.

"You don't know nothing about me, old man!" Antonio shouted, struggling to jump to his feet. The pain in his side took his breath away; and he doubled over. "That doesn't belong to you."

"I'm guessing I can say the same about that duffel bag of money." Cocking back the shotgun's hammer and waving the barrel, John gestured for Antonio to sit. "Like I said, I know what I need to," he said, tossing the dog tags back to its owner.

Without warning, the bedroom door burst open.

"Pops! Pops, you ok?" with Gabby at her side, Lana frantically searched the room for her father.

The stranger sat on the bed with his shirt open, his ribs wrapped with bandages, not uttering a word, as he stared into her eyes. The candlelight lit the sharp angles of his well-chiseled face.

"Girls, I told you to stay out there until I return," John growled.

"We heard all the noise and thought you needed us," Lana answered, with concern.

"Well, I'm fine. I'll be out soon." he said, not taking his eyes off their guest.

"Ok," Lana said reluctantly, as she slowly began closing the door while taking a last, long glance at the stranger in their house.

"Umph, he's even better looking cleaned up," Gabby whispered, as she leaned against the door frame.

"What do you know about good looks?" Lana said, giving her sister the side-eye.

"Enough," Gabby said, with a sheepish grin. "And I saw how he looked at you."

Lana rolled her eyes, "Whatever! Pops is right. We can't trust him, so stay away from him," she said, guiding Gabby away from the room.

Back in the room, Antonio quipped, "Nice family you have there."

"Now, that's something I don't want to hear come out your mouth," John barked, rising to his feet. "I will tolerate you, keep you warm and fed until this storm passes. But if you try to come near my daughters, I won't hesitate to put you down. Army or not. Do you understand?" he said, lowering the shotgun to his side.

"Ten-Four old man."

"I'll have some food and drink brought to you shortly," John continued, opening the door.

"Who should I call if I need something?"

"That would be me, John," he said, immediately closing the door, leaving Antonio cuffed to the bed.

9

John limped back into the kitchen, finding his daughters sitting around the small island sipping mugs of hot chocolate. Tossing the blade on the island, their eyes immediately fell on him, as he pulled a glass from the cupboard.

"What do you plan to do with him, Pops?" Lana asked.

Turning on the faucet and filling his glass with water, John removed a bottle of pills from his pocket. Opening the top, he tossed a couple of them into his mouth, and drank half of the water before setting the glass on the counter. He stared out the window, as it was being battered by heavy winds. Unconsciously, he massaged his knee while thinking about what to say to his daughters.

Turning to face them, "I'm going to do exactly what I said I would do. Keep an eye on him, and when this storm clears, contact the authorities. So for the time being, no one is allowed to go to him without my say so. He's a stranger and possibly a criminal, and therefore can't be trusted!"

"But to keep him cuffed to a bed, don't you think that seems a little harsh?" Lana added.

"Look!" John shouted, startling Gabby, causing her to spill a bit of her hot chocolate onto the island. Seeing his youngest daughter's reaction, he lowered his voice. "We don't know anything about him. He appeared at our door injured and in possession of a duffel bag full of money, possibly thousands of dollars. I have to assume the worst. My priority is the safety of the two of you only, not him."

"But Pops, we're better than this!" Lana pleaded, as she gently rubbed the pendant of a cat around her neck.

"Lana, I said what I said! No more debating. For now, I'd like you to take him some leftovers and something to drink, nothing more. And don't stay in there longer than need be. I'll be by the fireplace if you need me," he uttered and slowly exited the kitchen through a nearby door.

"What's wrong with Pops?" Gabby asked.

"Not sure. But Mom would never do this. Gabby, remember we always treat people with respect no matter what," Lana said, standing to prepare a meal for the guest.

"Yeah, yeah. Mom's golden rule."

****

Antonio contemplated his new dilemma, studying the dimly lit room for anything that could shed light on where he was. His first thought was to quietly drag the bed around, but that idea was promptly thwarted when he found it secured in place.

"There's that," he whispered to himself, then sat back on the bed.

Antonio sighed and leaned back into the pillows. His left wrist ached from the handcuff. *He didn't have to tighten them so much. How did I get here?* He thought. *Every time I think my luck is about to change, it does, but for the worse.* Just then, his thoughts were interrupted by a knock on the door.

Slowly opening the door to ensure he was still handcuffed, Lana found him lying on the bed. Stepping into

56

the room, she did her best to avoid eye contact with him, placing her focus on the tray of food she was carrying. With a few steps, she was at the nightstand by the bed and placed the tray of food upon it.

Antonio had only caught a brief glimpse of her before, but now in the flickering candlelight, he had more time to take her in. She appeared to be a little over five and a half feet tall. While she shared the old man's dark complexion, that is where the similarities ended. Her big brown eyes were focused on the floor, and her shoulder-length hair covered the right side of her face as she placed the tray down. She was curvy, not thin, but not heavy, just right. He found himself checking her out far longer than intended. His military training taught him to take in precise details quickly, but something about this woman made him pause.

Lana felt his eyes on her. Not taking her eyes off the tray, she snapped, "Didn't your mama tell you it was impolite to stare?"

Antonio snapped back, "Didn't your daddy tell you to speak when you enter a room?"
Silence hung heavy in the air, as Lana turned and made her way back to the door. Antonio grimaced; he did not mean for their interaction to go the way it did.

"Hey!" He called.

She turned around to face him, finally looking him in the eye, "Yes?"

He could see her whole face. Nope, she definitely did not look like her daddy. "Where am I?" he asked.

"A safe place," she replied.

"Yeah, it feels real safe." Antonio rolled his eyes and grimaced as he pulled himself up in bed. His ribs throbbed as if to remind him that he had miraculously survived a helicopter crash.

Lana's face broke with concern, "You should take it easy. From what I could tell, your ribs are badly bruised, but not broken. Sudden movements are going to hurt for a while."

Antonio sighed as he leaned back into the pillows, "You think?"

"Look," Lana continued, her voice soft, gesturing to the handcuffs, "That wasn't my idea, but we don't know you, or what got you here. This is how it has to be for now." And with that, she turned and walked out the door.

Outside Antonio's room, she took a deep breath. "That wasn't too difficult," Lana whispered to herself.

Peeking into the living room, she found her father dozing by the fireplace, the shotgun laying across his lap. She grabbed a blanket from the basket next to his armchair. She selected his favorite, the last one her mother crocheted, and draped it over him and the gun. With a smile, she bent over and kissed him on the forehead.

"Goodnight, Pops," she whispered.

10

The following morning, Lana awoke to the beeping of her alarm. Fighting the urge to fall back asleep, she reached for her cell phone and dismissed the alarm. It was 5:30 a.m. Growing up spending summers on the farm, her father taught her to be an early riser. It was a part of her now and had proven useful, especially in college.

In one slow but deliberate motion, she pulled herself up into a sitting position. With her feet hanging off the side of the bed, she eased on her slippers, grabbed her robe, and headed downstairs to the kitchen.

Lana had set the coffee pot to brew on a timer the night before. She could smell the aroma wafting through the air as soon as she began to descend the stairs. With sleepiness gone by the wayside, she couldn't wait to sip her first cup of coffee. She crept quietly, hoping not to wake anyone, as she stepped as lightly as she could on each step, trying to avoid making the stairs creek.

As she rounded the corner of the kitchen, she was tempted to check on Antonio, but she decided against it. Yet, that did not keep her from remaining silent to see if she could hear movement in his room. There was none.

Lana peered into the living room near the fireplace, her dad was still asleep where she left him last night in the chair, snoring softly. Black coffee with three teaspoons of sugar in hand, she crept back up to her room. Crawling back into bed, she opened her notebook and her Bible that she kept on her nightstand. Turning to the Book of James, Chapter 3:2, she read: We all stumble in many ways. Anyone who is never at fault in what they say is perfect, able to keep their whole body in check.

Resting the book upon her bent knees, Lana leaned her head back on the headboard, and thought about her conversation with Antonio last night. She felt bad about snapping at him for staring at her, maybe there was a better way she could have handled it, handled him. Her mom would always tell her that as her mouth moved, her sense was always trying to catch up—but this was, usually, right before she got in trouble. Lana chuckled at the memory of her mother.

Those sayings of hers: *Lana, you better get your mouth in check before your behind becomes collateral,* or *Baby girl, God loves you and I do too, but if you don't hush, you'll be meeting God sooner, rather than later!* Gabby would simply watch their verbal jousts like it was a tennis match, her head moving back and forth to see what each woman would say.

She felt her stomach knot up. A mix of conviction by the scriptures and memories of her mother. She would be more careful with her words and try to control her tongue. She continued to sip her coffee and meditate on the word of God. *Lord, lead me in my interactions with this man.*

"Mom, I wish you were here," Lana whispered, closing her Bible.

****

Hazy-gray light filtered through the curtains, stirring John from his sleep. He stretched his arms wide and let out a long, quiet yawn. He realized he had slept pretty well, considering he had spent the entire night sitting up, shotgun in hand. Looking around, everything appeared to be in its place. The blanket tumbled off his lap down to his feet as he sat upright. Taking in the blanket's warm colors and the fall theme that had been sewn into it, his eyes began to fill with tears, as he recalled the sweet memories of his beautiful wife, who had made this for him. Picking the blanket up, he gazed at it for a few seconds then laid it across the arm of the chair.

Gathering himself, he slowly made his way upstairs to his room to change clothes so he could start his morning routine—a routine that constantly reminded him of Gloria's absence. She used to set the timer on the coffee pot the night before so it would begin brewing the next morning. Since Lana was visiting, he knew she had already taken care it. The smell of coffee drifting through the house both comforted him and caused a lump to form in his throat. The bold aroma took him back to a time when he and Gloria would spend early mornings in the sunroom reading. It was something they did every day, both at the cabin and at home. He swallowed hard and the tightness in his throat eased, as he headed to the room he once shared with his wife.

At the top of the stairs, he opened the door to his bedroom. He'd often get a whiff of his wife's fragrance in the air, as if she were still here. He never completely understood it. Was his mind simply playing tricks on him? After all this time, a soft smell of a mixture of baby powder and Dove soap filled his nostrils, as he slowly inhaled, savoring the sweet scent of his wife. This was one of those days; it smelled like she'd just been in their room and had simply walked into another area of the house.

He sat on the edge of the bed, rubbed the tears away, and closed his eyes. He hoped that when he opened them, she would be there standing in front of him, as beautiful as she had always been. Yet, when he opened his eyes, reality continued to disappoint him. Her slippers were still at the foot of the bed. He could not bring himself to move them.

Lana had done most of the leg work, taking her mother's clothes off the hangers in the closet; but the bags of clothes were still there, waiting to be donated. He had promised to take them to the Goodwill, but every time he looked at the bags, he could not bring himself to do it. He shook the thoughts away as he got dressed, putting on his thermals in preparation for the blizzard-like weather outside.

Now dressed, he headed downstairs and slowly cracked open the door to Antonio's room. Seeing that he was awake lying on the bed staring back at him, John closed the door without saying a word. He walked into the kitchen and poured coffee into his thermos. Like any other day, he liked his coffee with no cream. Black, with just enough sugar to take the edge off. With his thermos in hand, he headed outside to chop more firewood, hopefully enough to get through the storm, and contemplate their current situation.

Chopping wood not only kept him physically fit, it was his means of staying busy and relieving stress. John opened the front door and stepped out into the frigid air, closing the door behind him. Pausing on the porch, he closed his eyes, and took a deep breath. It invigorated him, as he looked out at the beautiful, tree lined property. Snow covered the ground and the branches of the evergreens were weighed down by the white, powdery substance. He would never get tired of this view. He took another sip of coffee. After a few minutes, he put the cap on the thermos and grabbed the heavy ax that he left leaning near the cabin door.

With the shotgun in in his hand and the ax draped over his shoulders, John made his way around to the side of the cabin. He stopped in front of a large garage, with walls on three sides, except the front was opened. It could hold at least ten cars. Inside the prefabricated structure was large machinery once used to operate the family's corn business. Now covered with dust, rust, and chipped paint, the equipment sat idle, looking like metallic ghosts of the past.

John placed his thermos and shotgun on an old chair and leaned the ax against the stump of wood near him. He grabbed a piece of timber from a nearby wheel barrel, placing it upright on the stump. Grasping the ax and holding it at his side, he glared at the piece of wood as if it had done him wrong.

Taking a deep breath, he swung the ax as hard as he could, then paused briefly to gaze at the one piece of wood that quickly became two. He tossed them onto a pile. He placed another piece of timber on the stump. Repeating the ritual, John clinched his jaws and swung the ax with more fury than before.

"Why do you keep doing this to me? I came here to spend time with my daughters, and look at what you allowed to happen! Can't you just leave my family alone?" gritting his teeth as he brought the ax down with a loud thud, splitting the helpless timber.

"This is all your fault! It's always your fault!" he grumbled angrily, grabbing a piece of the timber from the ground, placing it back upon the stump for chopping. "If you only stayed out of my life, we would be enjoying each other as a family." His voice rising, as he split another piece of wood with a violent swing of the ax. He quickly tossed the two quarters into an already large stack of firewood. He promptly replaced it with another log, repeating the process several more times.

Taking a deep breath, he stared at it, "Now you have me playing babysitter. What gives you the right to continue doing this to my life?" John fussed.

"To do what, Daddy?" Gabby asked, stepping beside the stump, as she gazed at the puffs of steam heaving from his nostrils. She thought he almost looked like a mythological beast with an ax at his side.

"Oh, nothing, Gabby. I wasn't talking to you, sweetie," he said as he cleared his throat and quickly composed himself. "What, what brings you out here?"

"Well, I heard you leave the cabin earlier, and when you didn't return after a while, I came to check on you."

"I've only been gone for…" stopping mid-sentence, he glanced down and saw the large pile of chopped timber gathered around the stump. "Oh, I didn't realize I was out so long. Time got past me," he said looking up at her with a small smile.

"You ok, dad?" she asked, shivering in response to the chilly winds.

"I'm ok. No need to worry. But you go back in out of the cold, and I'll be in soon." With her gaze full of worry, Gabby relented and turned to head back to the cabin.

"Thanks to you, now my baby girl thinks I'm crazy," John grumbled, lining up another piece of wood, then quickly brought down the weight of the ax upon it.

****

Lana was hungry after finishing her morning devotional, so she ventured downstairs for breakfast. She found the house quieter than normal. She guessed her father must be outside chopping wood, being that is all he did since arriving. Gabby was probably in her room. *That girl could find ways to entertain herself on Mount Everest*, Lana thought with a smile.

She saw the pot of coffee was nearly gone, and she did not see her father's thermos in its normal place on the counter. Peeking out the kitchen window, she caught a glimpse of her dad carrying some chopped wood to the side of the house.

She walked over to the refrigerator and grabbed a carton of eggs, some bacon, Dutch scrapple, a type of meat pudding, and cheese. "An old-fashioned breakfast should change the mood around here," Lana muttered, sliding the cast iron skillet on the stove, and turning on the gas burner. She opened the breadbox to ensure Gabby had placed the bread in there when they arrived. Without it, they would not be having toast. Seeing the bread, she sighed in relief.

In a few minutes, she had the house filled with the unmistakable smell of bacon. Then she fried the scrapple in the bacon grease. Carefully pouring some of the excess fat into the dripping container on the counter, she left just enough bacon grease in the skillet to scramble the eggs. As the eggs bubbled up in the skillet, Lana took three slices of the cheddar cheese and placed it on top of the eggs. Watching the cheese melt, she scrambled the cheese into the eggs, seasoning them with just a touch of salt and some Italian seasoning. As the cheese eggs finished up, she sprinkled them with a bit of pepper and parsley. She smiled at the thought of her mother making this very dish not so long ago.

Having made enough food for all of them, even their guest, Lana fixed a plate with bacon, scrapple, eggs, and toast for Antonio, and placed it on a tray, along with a cup of what was left of the coffee, with sugar, no cream. She carried the tray to Antonio's door and knocked, balancing the tray with her free hand and hip. "Antonio, are you up?"

"Yeah, why?" he asked.

"Can I come in? I have breakfast for you."

"Yeah."

Lana inhaled deeply, then opened the door. She found Antonio sitting on the side of the bed, as if he was deep in thought. She was met with a familiar, pungent smell. "Oh god, what is that?"

Antonio gestured to the rusty bucket within reach of the bed. "Your old man wouldn't give me access to the head, told me to use that instead."

Placing the tray on the nightstand on the opposite side of the bed, Lana could feel anger and embarrassment boiling up. "Wait, he made you use a bucket?"

"I mean, yeah, but what do you care?"

Lana raised her hand, as if to say stop. She left the room, not closing the door behind her, and came back with gloves on and grabbed the bucket. She moved so fast Antonio did not have time to speak. He watched her, puzzled as she took long strides out of the door. With the bucket in hand, she took it down the hall to the bathroom and disposed of its contents in the toilet. He believed her disgust was not just at the human waste, but at her father. She returned to Antonio's room with a can of air freshener, spraying it throughout the room, but away from the tray of food.

"Damn, you alright?" Antonio asked.

Shaking her head, Lana just glared at him.

"You mad, huh?" He asked, reaching over to take a bite of the toast.

"Aren't you?" She asked, incredulously.

Antonio shrugged. "I mean, y'all don't know me. I'm basically a prisoner in your house. I get it."

"But you aren't some animal. Nobody should have to take a crap in a bucket!"

Antonio shrugged and took a bite of his eggs. He paused and looked at her, his eyes warm. "You make this?" he asked.

"Yes, why?"

"Damn girl, you put your foot in these eggs." The compliment shook away some of her anger.

"Uh, thank you."

"I haven't had a breakfast like this in years," Antonio said, taking a bite of toast and egg together. "And didn't your old man tell you not to come in here?"

Lana glanced at his wrist, which was still handcuffed. "What do you care?" She asked defensively.

"I'm just the prisoner," Antonio replied with a smirk, chomping on a piece of bacon.

"How are your ribs?" Lana asked, hoping to change the topic.

"They still hurt like hell, but thanks for the patch up," he continued.

"They will for a while," Lana acknowledged with a slight nod.

"Hey, how did you know they were bruised and not broken? You a doctor?"

"Yes, technically. I'm a veterinarian."

"Ah," he paused to take a bite of scrapple, chew, and look her in the eye. "So, you saw me naked?"

Lana could feel the blood rushing to her face, "What? No!" she said, shocked at his question. "I had to check your injuries though," she said looking down.

Antonio burst into laughter. Lana looked up and glared at him. "I'm sorry, I couldn't help it," he said, choking on his food between laughter.

Lana could not help but chuckle.

"So, a vet huh? I guess horses and humans aren't that different?"

"Oh, very different, but ribs are ribs. I can typically identify broken ones."

"What made you want to be a vet?" Antonio asked, sipping his black coffee, trying hard not to frown at the taste. *Where's the creamer? he thought. I ain't like old folks just wanting black coffee*, but he did his best not to show his dislike for it.

"I grew up spending summers on a farm. We used to have chickens, a few horses, a donkey...."

"Oh, so you had a *real* farm," Antonio interrupted.

"Yeah, we had—"

"Lana! Didn't I tell you not to come in here unless I told you to?" John's voice boomed from the doorway, as he gripped the shotgun tight, snow still falling from his coat.

Lana and Antonio both looked at John, whose eyes were glaring at them and nostrils flared as he looked back and forth from Lana to Antonio. He was livid.

"Lana, get out! NOW!" John roared.

"I need to speak to you anyway," Lana snapped back as she slipped past her father.

"I'll deal with you later," John growled at Antonio, as he slammed the door behind him.

Antonio shook his head, looking at his reflection in the cup and took another sip.

11

Lana walked with purpose into the living room of the Morris cabin.

Laying the shotgun across the coffee table and tossing off his coat, "What do you think you're doing?" John roared at his daughter.

Lana's blood was boiling, but she composed herself, as much as possible, because even though she was upset, she was raised not to be disrespectful to her parents. In a lower tone than what she'd normally use, she replied, "Pops, please don't yell at me. I was taking him food, that's all."

John was temporarily stunned by her measured response, but he was angry and would not be deterred. "What did I tell you, huh? Didn't I tell you not to go in there unless I specifically told you to? What? Now you're serving that criminal breakfast in bed?"

Lana's eyes flashed with anger, no longer able to keep her composure, as she quipped back. "Why? So, I wouldn't have to smell his urine and crap in the bucket you gave him?"

Gabby crept down the stairs and sat down out of view and listened intently.

"Lana, how can I protect you and your sister if you won't listen to me? We don't know what that man is mixed up in!" John paused, looking her in the eye. Lana returned his glare. "And I hate to break it to you, but in the field, soldiers didn't always have a toilet at their disposal."

"Pops, that would make sense if we were at war, but we're not! No, we don't know what he is mixed up in, but he showed up at our *home* hurt. He may or may not be a criminal, but he also needs our help. Is he our prisoner?"

"No! But he's not our guest either."

"This isn't how you and mom raised us, Pops. You're just going to pass judgment? No questions asked? What about the grace of God? What about mercy?"

"What about it? This is not an opportunity to meet your match Lana. This is real life. For all we know, he could be a serial killer," John snapped.

"Really, Pops?" Lana was incredulous, "That's a low blow." Her eyes filled with tears, "When you see my Pops, tell him I miss him, because I don't know who this man is standing in front of me."

Gabby stepped around the corner to make her presence known.

John looked up and saw matching faces of disappointment on his daughters' faces.

"Lana…Babygirl…I…I didn't mean…" John stammered.

Lana held up her hand as if to say stop, then sprinted up the stairs. Seconds later, Lana's door slammed behind her, startling John and Gabby.

John looked over at Gabby who was still standing there staring at him. To his surprise, she had tears in her eyes, as she walked toward him and silently wrapped her arms around him. He hugged her back and felt his heart break a little more, as her little body shook with tears.

"I'm sorry, I didn't mean…"

"Pops," Gabby sniffled, "It's not God's fault."

"What?" John easing his embrace of his youngest child so he could look down at her.

"It's not God's fault. None of it. I know that's who you're really mad at, and it's not His fault," Gabby said again, meeting her father's gaze.

John remained speechless as Gabby turned and headed up the stairs.

For a moment, John stood motionless and felt his anger start to subside. Looking towards the guest room, his anger was renewed. Heading to Antonio's room, his strides were strengthened by his anger.

John entered without knocking and without his gun. Simply by listening to the staggered, but quick steps approaching his room, Antonio knew the old man was pissed. *Here we go with the bullshit.*

"What happened between you and my daughter?"

"What do you mean? I've been handcuffed to the bed since yesterday! I ain't doing much of anything, as you should know," Antonio blurted, "except for the occasional shit in a rusty bucket," he said, raising his cuffed hand. Then he took the last swig of his coffee, put his cup down, and looked at John.

"What did you say to her?"

"Look, old man, I'm just biding my time until you turn me over to the police, unless you're trying to pull some shit, like in that movie, *Misery*, with James Caan."

"Don't use that language in my house."

"Whatever old man! You're the one keeping me prisoner here. And what, you some kind of saint, trying to save everyone around you? But instead of saving, you're screwing it all up! The main one who needs saving is you. Your daughter does the humane thing, and you disrespect her for doing so. From over here, it looks like you're the one who needs saving. Anyway, don't you guys always say, 'Do to others, what you want to be done to you?' Listen, John, I came here for help, and I got handcuffed. What makes you think I have my mind on anything other than getting out of here? I was trying to get free and look where I ended up."

John was jarred, reflecting on Antonio's words. He was not sure what he was anymore. In years past, he would never have talked to his daughters like that. They were everything to him. He walked over to the chair across from the bed. Now that his anger and adrenaline was wearing off, he could feel every subtle thump of pain in his knees. He gingerly lowered himself into the chair.

"So…what happened? How does one, such as yourself, end up here?" John asked.

"Oh, so now you want to talk?" Antonio asked, staring at John. "That's the sort of thing you ask first before cuffing someone to a bed."

"I agree, but I can't change that right now. What I can do is learn what happened. I want to know. Did you get caught up in some kind of criminal activity?" John pressed.

"Why do you assume that? Because I'm young and black?" Antonio shot back.

"I mean, if you haven't noticed, I am too, son. I mean, what am I supposed to think? You show up at my door half dead with a duffel bag filled to the brim with money," he explained.

"Look, I served my country, but my country hasn't served me." Getting agitated, Antonio sat up straighter in the bed. "I put my life on the line. I killed for my country. I saved lives for my country. And what did I get for it? A dishonorable discharge and having to deal with people like you!"

"What do you mean? I served my country too, in Desert Storm. I know what comes with the territory," rubbing his injured knee. "Yeah, this is a constant reminder of my past, and it's something I can't escape. And like me, I know you have things you can't escape. I also know you have to do something pretty horrible to get a dishonorable discharge."

"See, that's what I'm talking about. You just assume it must have been something I did. How about they needed someone to take the fall, and I was their token."

"Son, I am not a mind reader. Obviously, something went left. Instead of making assumptions about what I think, why don't you try changing my mind?" John said calmly.

Antonio changed positions so that he was sitting on the side of the bed. *Should I tell him what really happened?* The room grew silent.

John started to lift himself out of the chair.

"I was in Afghanistan," Antonio began, getting John to settle back in the chair. "I was in my bird and there had been some insurgent activity. I was providing overwatch for my soldiers on the ground. I saw a group of people that looked like they were hostile, and I made the call. Turns out it was a mix of civilians and friendlies. Given the conditions, it was a call that any experienced pilot could have missed. The friendlies were dressed like the insurgents to protect themselves. I nor the troops on the ground had any idea. Innocent people died that day. The upper brass was on my commanding officer's ass because of negative media coverage. They needed blood for blood. I was the sacrifice. Fifteen years of honorable service—gone with a dishonorable discharge stamp on my paperwork."

John took in what Antonio told him, shifting more into the chair.

"So, where did the money come from, son?"

"It wasn't mine, not all of it. I don't really know where it came from. A homeboy," Antonio looked up at John and adjusted his speech, "A friend of mine, he was looking out for me. My dishonorable discharge makes it hard to secure regular work. So he hit me up, uh, called me up about this job, someone needing a pilot. No details on who, just where the bird would be, and to wait for the package. Next thing I know, I see two guys with masks running toward me and hopping in the bird with two duffel bags full of money," Antonio paused.

"Well? What happened to the other two guys?"

"The storm came in, and the dude who appeared to be in charge, told me there's more pay for me if I keep flying through the blizzard. So I did. Nature wasn't having it. The bird went down, slamming into the ground, with us in it. I was knocked out for a bit, but I survived. The guy who apparently hired me died, probably on impact. The other guy is missing. I don't know if he was buried in the wreckage or if he somehow got out. But when I came to, only one duffel bag was there. So, I took it and whatever supplies I could gather. I don't know what happened to the other one. I climbed out of the bird and headed out looking for help. A few hours later, I ended up here."

John leaned in, looking Antonio in the eyes. "So, soldier, what were your plans for the money? Were you going to just take it and run?"

Now I'm back on trial again, Antonio thought. "You know what, man, I'm done," Antonio flipped his hand and waved John off before lying back on the bed. "If you don't mind, you can see yourself out. Holla at me when the police arrive."

John sat for a second looking at Antonio, and thinking about his bizarre story. Seeing that Antonio had shut down, John left the room.

12

John let out a long sigh, as he took a moment to gather himself outside of Antonio's door. He was tired. Even though it was only a little after noon, a lot had occurred. And his body was telling him he had pushed himself pretty hard chopping wood. With his knees slightly aching, he made his way to his bedroom.

In his room, John removed his top layer of clothes, and stripped down to his thermals, exhausted from the day's work, he laid down on his bed. As he let his body relax into the mattress, he reflected on his conversation. *How could it be so easy to slip back into counseling again? God, how can I minister to that young man when I don't even know if You still receive me?* Antonio's question still stung John, "What? Are you a saint or something?" *I don't know what I am anymore. And my girls, I don't know what they think about me. And Lana, will she ever forgive me?*

John felt the guilt settle like a stone in his stomach. It was heavy and uncomfortable. *Am I a hypocrite? How can I slip into ministry with Antonio after yelling at my own daughter?* John looked over at his nightstand where his worn, leather-bound Bible sat, a thin layer of dust on it. *Once upon a time, I thought all the answers were in that book. But now I know better.* John felt bitterness gurgle up, as he looked over to what had been Gloria's side of the bed. *If it wasn't His fault, whose fault was it?*

"Gloria, what have I become?" John wondered aloud. "I don't even recognize myself anymore. Without you, I've been lost. I abandoned the faith I swore to uphold. I even blamed God for your…your death." He inhaled deeply, holding back tears. "It wasn't the other driver's fault the road had frozen over. I had just turned my head to look at you—for just a moment. You were so beautiful. And then, just like that, you were gone. I…I needed someone to blame for you no longer being here with us, with me. Gloria, I was so angry…and it hurts more than any wound I received in service," John cried out, exhaling a choppy breath, and the tears began to flow. "But now I understand and see what I have to do. Will the Lord forgive me? Baby, will you forgive me?"

****

Gabby knocked on her sister's bedroom door, "Lana? Lana, it's me."

Gabby stepped back as Lana cracked open the door. "Can I come in?"

Lana hesitantly stepped back, allowing her to enter. Wiping away tears, she sat down on her bed, turning her head away, trying to avoid her sister's gaze. Gabby sat next to her older sister wrapping her in a loose hug. For a moment neither said a word, allowing the howling winds outside to speak on their behalf, and as Lana leaned into her, Gabby hugged her tighter.

Lana sniffled, "My, how the tables have turned," she said with a slight chuckle.

"Somebody's gotta be the grown-up around here," Gabby replied with a smile, still hugging her big sister. "And believe me, I'm going to make sure everyone remembers."

"Yeah, Pops and I weren't great examples, were we?" Lana asked, grabbing a tissue from the box on her nightstand. Blowing her nose, she released a trumpet-like sound.

"Ugh! I could hear the snot!" Gabby laughed, releasing her sister from the embrace.

"Better out than in, I always say," Lana replied, smiling despite herself. "No matter what, you manage to make me smile."

Gabby scrunched her nose up in feigned disgust. "I know. It's my mutant powers."

Lana looked at Gabby, her eyes were red from tears. Her smile faded.

Returning the stare, Gabby felt a lump form in her throat.

"I'm ok, Scooby," Lana said, patting her sister on the leg.

"Scooby? You haven't called me Scooby in years!" Gabby exclaimed, playfully punching her sister in the arm.

"Really? Maybe it's time I bring it back!" Lana replied, dodging another punch.

"I don't say, 'R'uh R'oh,' anymore," Gabby said, doing her best Scooby-Doo impression, while Lana burst out in giggles.

"Is it still your favorite cartoon?" Lana asked.

"Yes," Gabby replied sheepishly.

"I always thought you had good taste in cartoons," Lana replied while ruffling her sister's hair.

"So, are you going to talk to Pops first, or do I have to call you both on the carpet?" Gabby asked, changing the subject.

"What is there to say? He already KO'd me, Mortal Kombat style."

Gabby imitated the villain, Shang Tsung, "Flawless Victory!"

Lana couldn't help but laugh.

"But seriously, are you going to talk to him? I know what he said was savage, but he hasn't been the same since mom died. He's been…just…angry and sad," Gabby said, blinking away tears. "And whenever I try to help him, he acts like nothing is wrong."

"I don't know…to imply that something is going on between Antonio and I—what kind of person does he think I am?" Lana asked.

"Uh, one with a pulse!" Gabby replied chuckling.

Lana threw a pillow at her.

"Whatever. I was just being hospitable."

"Sure, you were. But um, if I was older, I'd be looking-looking," Gabby replied with a smirk.

Lana amply gave her the side eye.

"Side eye me all you want. You're saying you don't think he's cute at all?" Gabby asked.

Lana shrugged.

Gabby laughed.

"Are you playing dumb, so you don't have to lie to me?" Gabby asked, still laughing.

Lana could not keep a straight face, and soon joined in her sister's laughter.

Growing serious, Lana responded, "Look, I don't need that drama in my life. I've been through enough."

Gabby bit her lip, believing that she had pushed too much, "I'm sorry Lana. I didn't mean to bring up anything to make you think of…"

"Yeah, it's ok. I know I dodged a bullet." Lana replied.

"I guess," Gabby said with a shrug. "But it doesn't make it any easier," Gabby said getting up to leave the room.

"Scooby!" Lana called.

"Yeah?" Gabby responded, stopping in her tracks.

"Thanks for checking on your older sis," Lana said with a slight smile.

"Sure. And don't be too hard on the old man. Believe me when I say he's been better since you've been home," Gabby said, smiling at her sister, as she walked out of the room, closing the door behind her.

Lana stood and walked over to her jewelry box she had purposely left at the cabin. Inside was a gold band, with three tiny diamonds embedded. It had been a promise ring given to her by her high school and college boyfriend, Nate. They were going to get married, or so she thought. Nate got married alright, but not to her. Instead, he married the woman he fathered a child with while he and Lana were together. Lana let out a sigh. *Yep, I dodged a bullet.*

A knock from the door shook Lana from her memories.

"Uh, Babygirl, it's me," John said hesitantly from the other side of the door. "Gabby said I should come see you."

That girl, Lana thought, rolling her eyes. She was not ready to speak to him yet. She sighed as she responded, "Come in."

Entering the room with his head down, John was unsure of how to begin, "Look, Lana…"

"If you're here for round two, I don't have it in me, Pops," Lana replied wearily. Not taking her eyes off the ring, she twirled it in her hand and placed it back into the jewelry box. Then, she slowly turned to face her father.

"I'm not here to fight, Lana, I'm here to apologize. I said some things I didn't mean, and the last thing I want to do is hurt you. I…I'm just trying to protect you both. Lana, you and your sister, you're all I have left," John continued, his voice breaking. He coughed and composed himself.

Lana considered her father's words as she stared at him with compassion. She had not seen him this vulnerable since her mother first passed. She walked over to him and wrapped him in a hug. John felt something inside him break, and tears welled up in his eyes and rolled down his face as he cried uncontrollably, his body shaking, as if he were cold. Lana hugged him tighter. She had never seen her father shed more than a few tears, even at her mother's funeral. She felt her heartbreak a little with every shudder. After a few more moments, John pulled away, sheepishly. Lana handed him a tissue from the box on her nightstand.

"I keep them near for occasions such as this. I made use of them earlier." Lana smiled. "Pops, you know I love you, right?"

"I know. I'm sorry for getting all teary-eyed on you, I don't know what came over me," John replied, looking down at the floor.

"You don't have to apologize for your feelings, Pops. I'm sorry I haven't been around to support you. I was so caught up in my own hurt—I guess I just ran," Lana admitted, as she sat on the edge of her bed. Reaching out, she took hold of his hand. John lowered himself onto the corner of her bed.

"No, you had to go and pursue your career, Babygirl, I get that. I couldn't keep you home forever, no matter how hard I tried. You were always amazed and curious about what else could be out in the world," John replied.

"Yes, but I didn't have to go all the way to New York to do it. After everything that happened with Nate, I just couldn't deal with running into him with his family," she said with tear-filled eyes, fluttering her eyelids quickly, attempting to keep them from overflowing. "I needed a fresh start, but it shouldn't have come at the expense of you and Gabby."

John squeezed her hand, "I know Nathaniel hurt you some kind of bad. It's nothing wrong with taking some time to heal. You're grown, you didn't owe me or your sister anything. I'm your daddy. I got this."

Lana snatched a tissue from the box for herself and blew her nose loudly.

John couldn't stifle his chuckle, as Lana joined in on the laugh.

"So, we good, Babygirl?" John asked.

"Yes, Pops, we're good. I'm going to make some lunch. Would it be an issue if I included our guest in that number?" Lana added.

"Yes, but, Lana, be careful with him. We still don't know what he was up to with the money," John reiterated.

"I know, I know," Lana smiled.

"Ok," John said, smiling back. He patted her hand one last time, stood up, locked eyes with his Babygirl, nodded his head, and left the room.

For a moment, Lana remained sitting, taking in the moment, raising her head to the sky. "Thank you," she whispered, and headed downstairs to the kitchen.

<h1 style="text-align:center">13</h1>

Staring into the refrigerator, Lana searched for something to make for lunch. Her eyes fell upon the quarter loaf of bologna, and with bread in the breadbox, she knew exactly what to make. She also grabbed some slices of Sharp cheddar cheese and the butter. Looking in the crisper drawer, she pulled out lettuce and tomato. Finally, she took the mayonnaise and mustard off the refrigerator door shelf. Now that she had all of her ingredients, she closed the refrigerator door and grabbed the old iron skillet from the cabinet next to the stove.

"What are you making?" Gabby asked, skipping happily into the kitchen.

Lana turned toward Gabby and greeted her with a smile. "Something I know we haven't had in a long time."

Gabby glanced at the bologna on the counter. "Oh, ok, Martha Stewart," Gabby chuckled and headed to the living room.

Lana put the skillet on the burner and waited for it to get hot. She added a slice of butter and enjoyed the sizzling sound it made as it floated and spread out in the center of the pan. She sliced the bologna into thick slices and placed two in the skillet. There was room in the skillet to put two slices of bread to make them into toast, while the slices of bologna fried in the butter at the same time. Toasting both sides of the bread, she put them aside and continued to fry enough bologna for everyone to have one sandwich.

Lana hummed as she prepared breakfast for everyone. She grabbed four plates and placed them on the counter. Looking at the ingredients for the sandwiches, she felt like it needed something more. She knew exactly what it lacked. So, she decided to take it to the next level. Smiling, she decided to top it off with a fried egg. "Yes!" she said, happily. "Almost done," she quipped. Lana spread a little mustard and mayonnaise on each slice of bread, then layered it with fried bologna, cheese, and fried egg. She placed the lettuce and tomato on the side, like she had seen them do in restaurants. She stepped back, pleased with what she had done.

Although she loved working with and caring for animals, there was something special about being in front of the stove, which helped to calm her mind. Maybe it was the step-by-step motions to bring some sort of management to her life, or simply the savory smells. Either way, she found pleasure in it.

She placed two plates on the table for Gabby and her father. Then, she took out the tray, and placed Antonio's lunch on it. She paused for a moment, *I'm not sure if this is a good idea, but I guess I'll find out.* She lifted her plate up and placed it on the same tray with Antonio's lunch.

"Gabby, your plate's ready," Lana called to her sister in the living room.

Gabby walked into the kitchen, "Mmmm. Smells good," she said. Then, looking at the tray, she gave her sister a knowing smirk.

"What?" Lana asked.

"A lunch date, huh?" Gabby winked.

"No, I plan to leave his plate and take mine upstairs," Lana replied, feigning disgust.

"Uh-huh," Gabby replied, grabbing her plate and heading back toward the living room.

Rolling her eyes, Lana picked up the tray, walked to Antonio's room, and knocked on the door.

"Yeah," a voice answered from the other side of the door.

"It's me, Lana."

"Come in," he responded.

Lana shut the door gently behind her and glanced up to see him smiling at her. She paused for a second to take in the details of his chiseled face and perfect white teeth. Staring a second too long, she blushed, and quickly focused on the tray.

"Lunch already? I'm losing track of time," Antonio commented.

"Yeah, I bet. I'm sorry about that," Lana replied, putting his plate on the stand next to his bed.

Antonio looked at the sandwich, stacked with fried bologna, a slice of melted cheddar, cheese, and an egg on top, with the lettuce and tomato placed next to it.. His mouth watered, as he glanced over the beautiful display of food, and began assembling his sandwich.

Lana turned toward the door.

"Wait! I mean, you know, if it's ok. I'm not trying to get you in trouble with your old man. I feel like I haven't talked to anyone in a while," Antonio said, looking Lana directly in her eyes. *Meanwhile, maybe I can also get some information on how to get out of here.*

Thinking about what she should do, Lana thought it couldn't hurt to talk with him for a few minutes. So, she walked slowly over to the chair in the corner of the room, keeping her eyes on Antonio. She sat down with her plate on her lap, and took a bite of her sandwich. *Mmmm! That's good*, she thought.

"What's up with this storm?" Antonio asked, gazing up at the window. "The wind is crazy here. How long is it supposed to last?"

Lana swallowed her food prior to answering. "Before we lost reception, they were talking about it lasting for several days, at least. That's normal for this time of year, but I have to admit, this storm seems different than past years. Not sure if it's colder or the forces behind it. Either way, I can't put my finger on it."

"Shits crazy," Antonio added, getting a glare of disapproval from Lana. "My bad. That's crazy, even for me. And they say global warming ain't real." The room fell silent once more.

"Are you going to keep talking, or are you going to eat your sandwich?" Lana asked.

"My bad, it does smell and look delicious," Antonio said, taking a bite of his sandwich. "So, Miss Veterinarian, you also a Southern cook on the side?" Antonio said, taking another bite.

"What do you mean?" Lana asked, taking another bite of her sandwich. *Man, this is really good.*

"First, it was scrambled eggs, bacon, and scrapple. Now, a fried bologna sandwich with a fried egg and lettuce and tomato on the side? You're smart, and you can burn," Antonio replied with another smile.

"I guess you can take the girl out of the country, but not the country out of the girl," Lana shrugged, taking another bite. She peeked up and saw Antonio staring at her again, studying her intently.

"Didn't your mama teach you not to stare," Lana snapped looking him in the eye.

Antonio chuckled, "I apologize. In the military, you're trained to take in your surroundings—people, places, and things quickly. But, I can't figure you out with a glance."

Lana felt her face getting flush. "What do you mean?"

"Well, you're from here, but clearly spent some time back east. Your accent sounds like New York or New Jersey. You got Southern hospitality, but an East Coast attitude. But that's not the whole picture is it?" Antonio asked, watching her as he bit into his sandwich.

Lana subconsciously fiddled with the gold cat necklace she always wore. "You did pretty well. I'm actually from St. Paul. We come up here regularly, at least we used to—during the summer and for some holidays and breaks. But, I went to graduate school back east, and I'm still out there, in New York," Lana replied.

"St. Paul? For real? I grew up in Minneapolis!"

"Really?" Lana asked. "What a small world! We grew up just a few miles from each other."

"Small town girl heads to the big city, huh? I bet your pops is proud," Antonio said, taking another bite. *Damn, this sandwich is good. And damn, she sure looks good. Antonio, focus man!*

"Small town? C'mon, man." Lana said, rolling her eyes playfully, "Anyway, I'd like to think so. I didn't always plan to go so far away, but life kind of took me there," Lana shrugged.

"What do you mean?" Antonio asked.

Lana thought about if she should reveal the full reason, she headed east. Well, once this storm passes, she'd probably never see him again once he's handed over to the sheriff.

"I was engaged, and it didn't work out, so I needed a change of scenery," Lana said with a shrug, rubbing the cat around her neck.

"Oh, so the guys around here are stupid, really stupid," Antonio said, with a mouth full of food before continuing. "What happened?"

"Oh, so now you're digging, huh?" Lana asked.

"Look, I'm just wondering how a dude could be so dumb," Antonio responded, his eyes still fixed intently on her.

She sighed, "Well, he had a child with another woman, who he went on to marry."

"Word? Damn. I'm sorry," Antonio said, setting his sandwich down.

"It's cool." Lana shook her head and waved her hand absently as if waving the memory away. "He wasn't who I thought he was, and it was for the best. I went on to pursue my career, he went on to start a family."

"Ok, that's the textbook answer, but how long were y'all together?" Antonio probed.

"Wow, you are a super nosy, man. I didn't know guys were into getting the tea like women tend to be," Lana teased.

"As I said, I'm just trying to get a sense of who I'm dealing with," he said, picking his sandwich back up and taking another bite.

"Well, we dated from high school until the middle of our senior year of undergrad, so maybe close to eight years."

"So yeah, he was stupid, just stupid," Antonio said, shaking his head, "and since then?"

"What do you mean?"

"Anyone else special?" Antonio asked, eyeing her reaction.

"None of your business."

"So, I take it that means no," Antonio chuckled.

Lana rolled her eyes and laughed.

"Enough about me, what about you Antonio? Why are you here? What did you get yourself into?" Lana asked, sitting the rest of her food down to take in his answer.

Shit. Here we go, he thought. "What do you mean? You're not about to start on this same stuff your old man was on me about, are you?"

"No, I don't know what you and Pops talked about. But I don't think you are a criminal."

"You and your old man don't pull any punches, do you?"

"Please. Don't deflect. How'd you end up here?" Lana asked, not backing down and locking eyes with him.

Antonio took the last bite of his sandwich. Looking down, he stifled a belch. *What do I say?* Lifting his head, he found her still examining him, waiting for a response.

"Well?" Lana pushed.

He was not sure if it was her persistence or the allure of her eyes, either way, he found himself spilling the beans. Unlike with her old man, Antonio was not able to push back.

"Look, I was a pilot in the Army. I received a dishonorable discharge. That sh—excuse my language, that situation is comparable to being a felon. Whenever I apply for jobs and they run background checks, it pops up. It also makes it hard for me to secure housing. From there, it has just been a domino effect. So, when I was offered a job, I took it as a means to make some money to help my situation. Everything went FUBAR, as we say in the military, when this storm hit."

"What does that mean," Lana looked puzzled.

"Well, it means when a situation is so "fouled" up beyond repair, except we actually use a different "f-word," he chuckled. *I can't believe I just told her all that. Bruh, you slipping.*

"Dishonorable discharge?" Lana asked.

"Yep. I was the lucky scapegoat."

"Ok, I'll go with that. So what was the job?"

"Flying a chopper for a client. I didn't have any details except to pick up a package, then, drop the package off," Antonio replied.

Lana studied him. *He seemed to be telling the truth, but he is military, maybe he's trained to lie,* she thought.

"Hmmm," Lana mused aloud.

"Yo, I feel like you're interrogated me."

"No, I'm not. I'm trying to see where you're coming from. You see, unlike my father, I don't believe in handcuffing people to beds. But I'm not naïve either. I need to know what's up with you," Lana said, leaning back in the chair.

"There's the New York girl. Brooklyn, right?" Antonio asked.

"Yes. Alright, so I'll bite. There was a lot of money in that bag. So, you got caught up huh?" Lana asked.

Antonio looked down at the floor, "Something like that."

Lana studied him, what she saw was vulnerability. "Look Antonio, bad things happen, but it doesn't have to define your future. Instead of it being something that ends your life, it could be the jumping-off point for a new one."

"That's all very encouraging, Ms. Mayberry, but this is real life. It simply doesn't work that way," Antonio shot back.

Lana took a deep breath and composed herself. She remembered what her mom always said about her mouth moving faster than her brain.

"Alright, I'll eat that one. But I am talking about real life. There are so many examples of bad situations leading to a great life, you just have to keep pushing."

"Ok, Ms. Veterinarian, give me some. And I don't want to hear about Kansas's yellow brick roads," Antonio snapped.

"There's Joseph and how his brothers sold him into slavery. His own family did that to him, Antonio! He went on to become wealthy and became his family's saving grace."

"The Bible? You talking 'bout in the Bible, Lana? That's all you got?" Antonio asked with a chuckle.

"Oh, so you don't think that's real life?" Lana asked.

"Once upon a time, maybe, I believed that could be true. Then, I realized those were just stories to encourage the weak," he said, bitterness creeping into his voice.

"Ok, I'll give you a 'real-life' example." Lana continued, "Me. Antonio, I lost who I thought was the love of my life, and my mother, who was my very best friend, in about two years of each other. The only thing I had to hold onto was my faith. I went to a place that was foreign to me and had to essentially start over. I was able to take those bad situations which could have made me bitter and complacent, but I was able to get my life together and move forward by leaning on God."

Antonio rolled his eyes.

Lana paused, *Lord, please give me wisdom for how to handle this man. I feel like I'm falling flat.*

Lana changed gears, "So a dishonorable discharge, is it really like being a felon? I mean, you served our country."

"Look, generally a dishonorable discharge means someone did something wrong or illegal to be put out of the military. It can be anything from going AWOL to murder. None of those things is a good look for potential employers. I've been in the military since I graduated from high school. I left my auntie's house, supporting myself for about fifteen years. Now, I'm right back at my auntie's house, sleeping in my old bedroom. And can you believe I have a curfew?" he said with disdain. I'm thirty-three years old. I mean, what does that look like for a grown man, huh?"

"Your aunt's house?" she said, furrowing her eyebrows. "What happened to your parents? Why aren't you living with them?" Lana asked. The room fell silent. She was not sure if he had enough of her interrogation and was simply shutting down. But she felt like she needed to ask, needed to know.

Antonio's faced became solemn, he looked down at the floor again. "They died my freshman year of high school. My mom's sister took me in. Got me through high school. She's good people. Not many would take in a knucklehead like me. Especially since she'd already raised her kids."

I'm so sorry," Lana said, looking him in the eye and clasping her necklace.

"It is what it is, you know? I guess God saw how good they were and thought they'd do better with Him than me," Antonio shrugged.

Lana felt a lump form in her throat. She didn't know what to say.

Antonio noticed Lana's hand had not left the gold cat necklace.

"What's up with the necklace?"

"Oh," Lana said, becoming self-conscious and releasing the necklace. "My mom sent me this right after FeFe died."

"FeFe?"

"FeFe was the cat Pops originally bought for my mom. He had forgotten their tenth wedding anniversary. He named the cat FeFe, as a reminder—forgive everyone, for everything. My mom couldn't help but laugh when Pops told her what the cat's name meant. I tell you, that cat tested her on that principle nearly every single day. FeFe was a jerk to my mom, always hissing and scratching at her. That cat became more like my dad's cat than my mom's. And when I was born, apparently, FeFe bonded with me, always sleeping near my crib, and being super gentle and patient with me. So, she became my cat. She died while I was away at school. That was around the same time everything went downhill with Nate, my ex. On the back of my cat necklace, it says, 'Forgive everyone, for everything.' It helped me let him go."

"So, it's safe to assume your family is Christian?" *This is my opening.*

"Yes, we were always active in church. My pops was a deacon."

"So, this," Antonio said, raising his handcuffed arm, "is this a part of your faith?"

"No! Not at all. It is a part of a father trying to protect his family. I'm sorry about this, but I understand why my pops did it." Lana replied, taken aback.

"Really? You said earlier, you didn't believe I needed to be in handcuffs," Antonio replied. *Got her.*

Antonio continued, "You don't have to feel sorry for me. What do you know? You grew up on a farm," he said sharply. He immediately regretted it. *That was probably too far.*

"Look. Nobody feels sorry FOR you, I am sorry for this situation, "Lana quipped, then, continuing, "And you're not the only one who has had hardships."

"Oh, really? Thank you for that after school special."

"One thing can make your life harder, yes, but it sounds to me like you kept messing up," Lana snapped, and abruptly stood up. "And for the record, you're not the only one who has lost the life you planned for yourself. Things happen in life, even to good people," she said, as she walked toward the door.

"Look, please, wait," Antonio said, looking down and holding up his cuffed hand.

"What?" Lana asked, arms crossed.

"I'm a captive audience," Antonio said, smiling.

Lana felt the chuckle tickling her lips, which quickly evolved into a belly laugh.

Antonio started laughing as well, until he winced in pain and began coughing. "Damn, forgot about these ribs."

Lana rushed to his side and stopped short. "Um, may I?"

"What?" Antonio asked.

"Can I check your ribs again?

"Uh, sure. I guess."

"Lay back, please," Lana instructed. She gently lifted his shirt. She gently removed the bandages, forcing herself to ignore his defined abs. She turned her focus to his ribs on the right side; they were black and blue. "I'm going to touch you, ok? Just going to make sure they're healing properly."

"Ok," Antonio paused, and held his breath. There was a slight chill in the air. Her hands were warm and soft on his skin. *Baseball, basketball, Kobe Bryant, Black Mamba...nope, my Mamba needs to chill. Nope. Football. Touchdown...Nope.* "Ow!" he said, grimacing.

"I'm sorry. The bruising looks worse. I think you need to see an actual people doctor soon," Lana said, pulling his shirt down. He gently grabbed her wrist. Lana felt a thrill go through her whole body. Antonio paused; he could feel her heart racing through her wrist. She was close enough that he could smell her, a mix of Dove soap and a hint of the food she'd made for them.

Lana cleared her throat. "Can I have my wrist back, now?" Her voice was lower and not as sharp as she intended.

Antonio ran his thumb over Lana's pulse in her wrist and tried to make eye contact with her before releasing it. But she avoided his eyes and gently pulled away.

Lana's breath caught audibly, as she tried to breath normal. She refused to meet Antonio's stare as she quickly headed for the door. *Shoot!* Lana thought. *Pops is probably wondering what's taking me so long to come out of this room.*

****

In the meantime, John and Gabby sat in the living room admiring the snow falling outside the window, while enjoying the ambience of the warm fireplace. With the past few days of the blizzard, about three feet of snow had accumulated outside.

Suddenly, there was a loud pounding on the front door, the sound carrying all the way through the house. It startled John and Gabby.

"Who could that be?" John wondered aloud.

"In this weather, not sure, Pops. Do you think maybe it's Officer Blake checking on us again?"

"Hmmm, I don't know. This snow makes it hard for any vehicle, other than a snowmobile to get around," John muttered, lifting himself out of the chair to answer the door.

Without looking through the peephole, John opened the door.

"How are you Officer—," John's words were cut short upon seeing a six-foot guy standing in front of him with a black ski mask covering his head and face.

"Who are you?" John roared.

"I don't want no trouble, old man," a male voice barked.

****

As Lana stood by Antonio's bedroom door, she thought she heard a loud knock and voices coming from the living room. Whose voice is that? she whispered out loud. She glanced inquisitively at Antonio.

Antonio recognized that voice. Shit! Lana, wait! Don't go out there!

Lana froze, hearing the urgency in Antonio's voice!

14

John looked his uninvited guest over, taking in the fact that the person had broad shoulders, indicating it was male. He was alarmed when he caught sight of a dark, metal shape just beneath the man's parka. It was a partially concealed weapon, that looked like some sort of submachine gun.

"Who are you?" John asked firmly, but being careful to speak calmly since this man was armed. He turned to glance at Gabby, whose eyes were bulging wide with a puzzled look on her face.

"Look, old man, I'm going to get straight to the point. I'm looking for someone who I tracked here." The man replied with a harsh, low bass which immediately put John on edge.

Tracked? It would take some serious talent to track through these conditions, John thought. "You didn't answer my question, who are you?" John said again, his voice rising, sounding even more firm, blocking the doorway with his body, as he again glanced over at Gabby.

Gabby took that as her cue to get somewhere safe. She slipped quietly out of the living room, just out of sight of the doorway. Her eyes shot toward Antonio's door, knowing Lana had taken him something to eat before the stranger came. Reaching the room without being seen from the doorway was going to prove to be a challenge. For her first move, she crept as quietly as she could to the kitchen.

"Ok, Gabby, what to do? What to do?" she questioned herself, hands in the air, bouncing her finger as if playing an imaginary piano. "I know, I know. Pops has guns, she whispered with excitement. But, soon sounded deflated when she remembered that he kept the guns in a locked cabinet. "Come on. Come on," she said. "There are only three places the key could be, and I bet Lana knows where it is."

Back at the front door, the man was becoming tense. John glanced at the gun resting by the man's hip.

"Look, I don't know who you are, old man, and I don't care. All I need to know, is if there is a man here who survived a helicopter crash? If so, he has something that belongs to me. His tracks lead this way, so don't even think about lying," he said, flipping his coat open to reveal the MP5 submachine gun.

John knew the MP5 is a tactical submachine gun capable of spewing hundreds of rounds per minute. At close range, it could easily decimate anyone. All he could think about was how to try and keep his family safe.

"Who are you?" John roared, ignoring the threatening prompt. "Never mind, I don't care who you are, leave my property, now!" he barked, turning his body slightly to be in a defensive position.

"Fine, then we can do this my way." Without hesitation, the man lunged at John, attempting to force his way into the house.

John anticipated the move and swerved his body a bit to the right going with the man's push, throwing the man off balance. He immediately countered, by giving the man an open palm strike to the chest. And before the man fell completely backward out of the door, he grabbed John, sending them both falling into the snow drift.

****

The commotion put both Lana and Antonio on alert.

"What in the world?" Lana asked, looking at the door. Antonio, I need to go and see what's going on. I need to make sure my father and Gabby are alright. Something is wrong.

"Shit! Lana, you need to listen to me. If you want your family to get out of this safe, you have to let me go." Antonio said, feeling the adrenaline begin to rush through his veins.

"What do you mean? Do you have something to do with this?" Lana asked.

"Yes and no. I'm pretty sure that's part of the package I was supposed to drop off before my chopper went down in the storm," Antonio replied, pointing at the door.

"What?"

"That voice, that was one of the men I was supposed to pick up and drop off with the money. He's a bad dude, Lana. He will kill all of us for that duffel bag!"

The realization of what was happening hit her as she peeked out the bedroom door, which had a clear line of sight to the front of the cabin. The door was wide open and all she could see was a white haze whirling into the cabin like an angry dog searching for an intruder.

She slid out of the door without another word to Antonio. She knew her father kept the keys to the handcuffs in the same case as the keys to the gun cabinet. Peeking

105

around the wooden post near the door, she nearly screamed out when Gabby emerged out of the shadows.

"You scared me half to death, Gabby!" Lana whispered, taking in deep breaths. "Where's Pop?" What's going on? Who was banging on the door?

"I don't know. Some man was banging on the door. I don't know who he is. He was talking mean to Daddy, and they got into it. I think they're outside fighting in the snow!" Gabby said, her eyes wide with fright.

"Oh my, God!" Lana shrieked under her breath. She took a few seconds to think and calm herself in front of her younger sister. "Ok, I'm going to get the keys to the handcuffs and the gun cabinet. Go in the room with Antonio and shut the door," Lana ordered, pointing toward the bedroom door.

Gabby ran into the room without another word. She locked eyes with Antonio, before quietly closing the door behind her.

The gun cabinet was in the formal dining room, across from the living room, but on the other side of the front door. Lana crept along the left wall, and unlike movies, their lives were in real danger. The keys were in an old Crisco container in the pantry, across from the kitchen. Peeking toward the door, she saw two figures struggling in the snow, the stranger tried to get on his feet, but her father wrestled him back to the ground, until he was once again covered in snow.

When Lana reached the pantry, she looked over her shoulder to make sure the coast was clear. She stepped inside and stood on her tiptoes, grabbing the Crisco container on the top shelf. She was relieved to find both sets of keys in there. Just then, a howl of pain echoed from outside the front door, causing Lana to freeze in place. Initially, her heart skipped several beats, believing it was her father screaming. But she promptly put that thought to rest, as she realized the yell came from someone who sounded much younger. With keys in hand, she peeked out the pantry door, making sure it was safe to come out. She knew she had to get Antonio free first. But before taking another step, she stood still, listening for footsteps or any noise indicating someone was in the house. As her eyes darted around, she did not see or hear anyone else in the house, which was a good sign. She crept quietly back to Antonio's room.

She knocked softly and opened the door, as she whispered, "It's me!"

Gabby and Antonio were already standing by the door.

"How did you get free?" Lana asked him.

Shrugging his shoulders, Antonio pointed to Gabby.

"I found Pop's spare key," Gabby replied sheepishly.

"That's ok, good thinking. Antonio, my dad has a gun cabinet in the formal dining room. Follow me, I have the key," Lana said, turning back toward the door.

"No. You need to stay here with your sister. Give me the key," Antonio whispered, holding out his hand.

Lana paused, looking at Antonio, as she thought, *Can I trust him?*

"Look, you're going to have to trust me, Lana, we don't have time to debate. Give me the key!" Antonio said more forcefully.

"So, what, I'm supposed to wait here and trust a stranger to save my father? Besides, I know my way around guns. I was raised on a farm after all," Lana said, absently taking his hand.

"Fine," Antonio continued, shaking his head, allowing her to lead him to the door.

"Gabby, hide in the closet." Lana directed her sister.

"I tried calling the police, but there's still no signal," Gabby added.

"Yeah, but we both know they wouldn't get here in time anyway," Lana said. So, please, hide. You know there's the little hatch in the back that opens to the crawl space. Get in there. If we don't come back, stay there until it's quiet, then follow it out. No one will think to look there, you're the only one still small enough to fit in there," Lana said, with a reassuring smile, letting go of Antonio's hand to give her sister a quick hug.

"Go and be quiet," Antonio said, nodding at Gabby as he pointed to the closet. "If we're going to help your father, we need to go now."

Lana released her sister and took Antonio's hand. Before exiting the bedroom, she turned and watched as Gabby made her way into the closet. And with her being safe for the moment, Lana's thoughts went to her father. She led Antonio along the wall toward the formal dining room. It was then that they heard another howl of pain, but this time there was no doubt it was her father. She gripped Antonio's hand even harder, pulling him so they could move faster.

"You know, I'm not a child. You don't have to hold my hand," Antonio quipped, holding up their hands.

"I'm sorry," Lana replied quickly, dropping it, and shrugging. "We need to get to my father. I think he's hurt."

"I know," Antonio whispered, switching places so Lana was behind him.

"The formal dining is to the left of the doorway," Lana directed him, following close behind.

They both turned along the wall into the room, glancing back to make sure the bad guy was not in the house. Lana gestured toward the back of the room, as she rushed to the gun cabinet and unlocked it. She quickly pulled out her father's .357 magnum and the double barrel shotgun.

"Which one do you want?" she whispered.

He looked at her incredulously. *Damn, she wasn't playing.* "I'll take the Magnum."

Lana handed him the gun and a handful of loose rounds from the cabinet; which he stuffed into his back pocket.

Even in the dire situation they were in, Antonio could not help but take in the weapon's craftsmanship. Its appearance was a sleek black matte, with smooth angles. Glancing over the Taurus .357 as it balanced perfectly in his hand, he realized that her father had it personalized with an cight-round cylinder, instead of the traditional six. Opening the cylinders breach, he found it already loaded. *Hmph! Not just a grouchy old man after all.*

After taking in the weapon, he glanced over and watched as Lana made intentional movements. She proceeded to load the shotgun with precision, having the breach opened and both rounds loaded in seconds.

Antonio had to look away to focus. *Man, if this wasn't a life and death situation, I'd be turned on. This woman is smart, can burn, and load a shotgun like the Terminator. Sexy, yet terrifying.*

He heard the click of metal as Lana finished loading and closed the shotgun's breach.

With his eyes and weapon focused on the door, "You stay out of sight for now," Antonio directed Lana.

"I'll stay out of sight as much as possible, but I'll be watching from the window," Lana replied with a nod.

"I hope you can shoot as well as you can cook," Antonio quipped, stepping towards the open door.

"Better," Lana replied, her face intense and focused.

Antonio could not resist a smirk as he stepped toward the door. It quickly faded as the wind hit him, the frigid air was sobering.

Here we go soldier, Antonio mused, quietly slipping out the door into the thick blanket of snow.

15

John and the stranger continued to tussle, landing in the deep snow again, with a soft thud. As they tumbled around in the cold substance, each trying to get the upper hand, the snow quickly enveloped half their bodies. During their scuffle, John did his best to keep the man's hand from reaching his gun as they rolled and tumbled around.

Suddenly, the stranger broke free of John's grip and quickly made it to his knee. Changing his tactics, the stranger let out a loud animal-like sound, as he threw a punch with all his might, aiming straight at John's jaw.

With his heart pounding hard, John pushed up with all of his might and managed to get up on one knee. Not being as fast as he used to be, he attempted to dodge the hammered fist he saw flying toward his face, quickly turning away. The blow landed hard on his shoulder, stunning John. It had been years since he had taken a blow like that, and feeling the impact and strength behind it, he was sure if it had connected with its intended mark, he would be lying face down in the snow. It was also clear the stranger's size and weight were not for show. This guy was a brawler, and if John were to stand a chance, he needed to end the scrimmage or evade quickly.

Adrenaline and years of military training kicked in as John did his best to shake off the punch, quickly returning one of his own, hitting which the mark—the man's midsection. The stranger doubled over and howled in pain.

The punch seemed to hurt him much more than John had expected.

He must have a previous injury, John thought. *This is my window, now or never.*

With the brief pause in their brawl, both men glared menacingly at each other, taking in deep breaths of cold air. John quickly assessed the situation, stood up, and looked down at his kneeling adversary. He snarled at the stranger, then threw a haymaker toward his face to end the fight.

But this time the stranger was ready and rolled beneath the punch, completely avoiding contact with the old man's fist, just like he planned. This move put him behind John.

I didn't expect that, John thought and tried to quickly change his position.

But before he could react, the stranger immediately put him in a chokehold and leaned back to raise him off his feet.

Using all the strength he could muster, John fought to free himself, but his fight was futile. It was difficult to breathe, John tried to regain his footing, which was crucial to get out of this mad man's grip. With each passing second, John knew he was in trouble. He could feel the grip tighten around his neck every time he tried to inhale and exhale.

"Nice moves, old man, but it ends now," the stranger whispered in John's ear, his breath hot and putrid.

John started to feel the effects of oxygen deprivation in his body, his knees began to buckle. If he did not react soon, he knew that he may never wake up again; however, the thought of not knowing what would happen to his daughters invigorated him. Reaching overhead, he used his thumbs to gouge at the man's eyes. The stranger roared in anguish, pushing John away.

Gasping for breath upon his release, the cold air was welcomed and filled his lungs. Although the pressure on his neck only lasted for a few seconds, to John it felt like an eternity. Once he caught his breath, he realized he came out of the chokehold with more than a breath of fresh air. John looked down and saw that he had the man's black ski mask in his hand. That is when he heard the sound all soldiers never want to hear. It was the *click* of a weapon chamber being loaded with a round.

John's heart seemed to stop, shocked by this change of event. With his hands raised, he was greeted with the barrel of the MP5 muzzle aimed at his face. But his attention was not on the weapon, he had seen that before. His focus was on the man behind it. The man's eyes were as green as algae in stagnant water and pockmarks covered his olive skin, as he gave a devilish smirk.

"So, what's going to happen..."

Before John could finish his sentence, the stranger quickly turned the butt of his gun and slammed it into John's bad knee.

"*AHHH,*" John cried out in pain, stumbling backward, falling into the blanket of snow beneath him. "AHHHH!" John continued to holler, gripping his knee, and rolling back and forth in the snow.

"See, old man. I told you I didn't want no trouble. But now, you've pulled off my mask. So, trouble you got. Now, get up on your broken knee and take me to my money!" The man growled.

With his gun still aimed at John, the stranger saw movement. Quickly glancing over his shoulder, he saw Antonio. "Nice for you to join us. Was starting to think, you'd skipped the party."

"Lester, let the old man go," Antonio said firmly, pointing the gun at the man's back.

"Sure thing," as he bobbed the gun up and down pointing at John, then pivoted to look at Antonio. "Soon as you give me my money."

"I don't know where it is, but he does," nodding at John. "Dead men don't talk, do they? So, if you kill him, we'll never know. So, let him go."

Silence fell over them, except for the sound of trees groaning under the wind's bombardment.

"There's truth in that. Get up, old man," Lester ordered.

John slowly began to lift himself up, then collapsed back into the snow. "I don't think I can walk on my own," John grimaced with clenched teeth, grabbing his knee.

Antonio paused. *This guy doesn't know about Lana, which gives us a defensive advantage. But taking him in the house will expose them all.*

"Tick tock, soldier boy, I got money to collect," Lester taunted, turning back to face John.

Before Antonio could decide what actions to take, Lana came running out the door, hands raised in surrender, kneeling at her father's side.

In one smooth, quick motion, the man switched targets.

"Who the hell is this? he demanded, his barrel trained on her.

"This is my father," Lana cried out. "Please, let me take him inside. I can get your money."

Hmmm…the man mused audibly, giving Lana the once over while sucking his teeth. "You sure don't look like your daddy, girl," he said, revealing a slight Southern drawl.

Lana felt disgust curdle in her stomach, feeling herself being undressed with his gaze. Somehow, she managed to keep her emotions from showing on her face.

"Please, just let me take him in," Lana asked, cautiously looking up at him. "We don't have anything to do with your money."

"Anyone else I need to know about?" The man asked, shouldering the weapon to aim at Lana.

"Hey! Hey!" Antonio cried out, taking a couple of steps forward, ready to pull on the trigger.

"Don't get your panties twisted up boy," he laughed. "I wouldn't hurt this perfect specimen," he said, as he smiled down on her.

"No, no. It's just me," Lana assured him.

He glanced at Antonio and looked back at Lana, thoughtfully for a moment.

"Alright! Go ahead. Get your dad up, and then bring me my money. In fact, maybe I'll go in with you to get it," he said with a wink.

"Naw, man! Damn that!" Antonio interjected. "It's not going down like that. They'll get your money, then you go. No time spent."

"Hmph," the man snorted, "That's all I came for anyway," he said, shrugging his shoulders. "Playtime can wait for another day."

He watched Lana intently, as she bent down to help her father stand to his feet. He made a motion as if he was about to reach and touch her, then looked over at Antonio who still had his gun trained on him. He smirked, as Antonio composed himself.

"I would give up my share too, if she was part of the deal."

"You just watch your eyes and keep your hands to yourself, or you'll get more than money," Antonio said through clenched teeth.

Lana leaned down and put John's arm over her shoulder.

"Ok, Pops, on the count of three, you try to lift yourself. I got your side," Lana instructed. "One, two, three," she said, and they stood up together with a grunt.

"Betsy?" John whispered, beneath the howling winds.

"She's just inside," she whispered back.

Betsy is what they all called the oldest of John's guns, the double-barrel shotgun. Betsy had been John's father's gun and was nearly as old as the cabin itself.

"You've got a minute to bring me my money, or I'll start shooting," Lester cautioned Lana, as she and John trudged up the steps and entered the cabin. The intruder quickly transitioned his aim from John and Lana to Antonio.

Lester and Antonio trained their eyes on each other.

"You're a hard man to find, Antonio"

Antonio shrugged, "Unfortunately, not hard enough."

"I'm surprised you survived that crash; it was a helluva ride, but weak individuals usually don't survive shit like that."

"Same could be said for you," Antonio replied, his finger gently resting on the trigger.

"I have to say, this is a nice place. How much you think they'll sell it for?" the man commented, as the snow swirled around them.

"Cut the small talk, you sick bastard!"

"Whoa, whoa, whoa! Why the harsh words? We are partners after all. Because of you, my pot is a little bigger, so good job on the flying. Sorry, Brad had to die for it to happen. But that's the way the Almighty wanted it, right?" he said, lifting his free hand to the air as if waiting for others to agree.

"God had nothing to do with this. Naw, this is the result of you two being greedy and trying to force your way through a snowstorm. I just happened to get caught up in it," Antonio argued; and then they both fell silent again.

A second or two later John, with Lana's help, returned to the doorway, tossing the duffel bag onto the porch next to Antonio's feet.

Antonio glanced at the bag; his gun trained on Lester. Stooping down to retrieve it, he heaved it as far to the left of his adversary as possible.

"There's all the money," Antonio said, gesturing to the duffel bag. "Take it and go!"

The man eyed the bag and looked back to Antonio, with a sinister smile on his face.

Shit. He doesn't plan to just leave, Antonio thought, glad that he already had one bullet in the chamber.

"That was the plan…then the old man had to take off my mask."

Knowing what was coming, Antonio turned and yelled, "In the cabin, now!" Immediately, Lester pulled the trigger, releasing round after round towards the cabin.

Lana dove onto John, sending them both tumbling to the floor just inside the cabin door. Wood chips, glass, and splinters flew in every direction.

Antonio narrowly managed to dive behind the waist-high solid oak railing that wrapped the front porch, as bullets soared past where he had just stood.

With everyone behind cover, the stranger grabbed the bag and immediately started running.

Hearing the break in fire, Antonio rose and returned fire. The magnum roared to life, echoing like a cannon off the surrounding woods. His target began dodging side to side in the snow, avoiding the incoming fire, causing Antonio to hit nothing but distant trees. As Antonio lined up his last shot, Lester disappeared around the side of the cabin.

"FUCK!" Antonio cursed at himself. With his weapon nearly empty, he promptly reloaded. Having it ready, he paused briefly at the cabin's door and peered inside. "You guys ok?" he asked, seeing Lana and John picking themselves up off the floor.

"Yeah, I think so," Lana answered, nodding.

Hearing that good news, he headed down the stairs, through the snow and woods, after their attacker.

16

Antonio could not believe he managed to get into a shootout after being out of the service for the last few years. Being broke and struggling had become the norm, but protecting a family he did not know from Adam was completely out of left field. He could not help but shake his head in disbelief as he approached the corner of the cabin.

With his back against the cabin and the magnum held at low ready near his chest, he cautiously peered around the corner, when suddenly, a hail of gunfire erupted, the deafening sound seeming to pierce his eardrums as the bullets tore into the wooden beams where he stood, forcing him to pull back and take cover. The roar of the MP5 was deafening, and if Antonio planned to end the fight, he had to close the distance somehow.

Taking in his surroundings, he noticed a large pile of chopped wood six feet from his position. He took a few paces back and sprinted as fast as he could, the sound of his rapid breathing echoing in his ears. Breaking line of sight at the corner, his adversary's submachine gun blared to life. Rounds were so close, he could hear them whizzing by, and at the last second, he dove and rolled. Landing behind a pile of wood, he immediately checked for injuries. Besides sore ribs, a snow-soaked shirt, and wind stinging his exposed skin, he was fine.

More rounds began pelting the stack of wood near Antonio's head, sending large splinters flying his way, as he threw his arms up to block them from causing any damage.

"Why'd you go and make this personal, Antonio? It's just business," Lester yelled from his position on the other end of the cabin. When Antonio didn't answer, he pressed the trigger, sending rapid fire into Antonio's hiding place, wood chips spraying everywhere. Then, nothing! "Damn! I'm dry," he said between gritted teeth, his magazine empty.

The logs gave Antonio multiple angles to return fire. Hearing the click, and then the silence, he took to one knee and leaned around the right side of the pile, squeezing off three rounds, interrupting Lester's reload, forcing him to fall back into the open-air garage. Capitalizing on the moment, as Lester reloaded, Antonio stood and followed suit to close the distance.

"Hey, Antonio, how about we call this quits, huh? No need for us dying and losing a chance at this money. It'll be a waste," Lester negotiated, taking cover behind the large tractor wheel. Greeted with only the howling of the blowing wind, he peered out and caught a glimpse of Antonio entering the opposite end of the garage. "Why the silent treatment, Bro?" he asked, immediately stepping out to unleash a barrage of bullets.

Ducking behind a rusted-out John Deere Corn Harvester, sparks showered all around Antonio, and he promptly fired several shots back before retreating to take cover. Opening the magnum's chamber, he reached in his back pocket for rounds to reload, only to find three.

"Awe, this can't be happening," he whispered, searching around at his feet, then back out at the woodpile. *Must've lost them when I rolled behind that pile.* "What to do now?" he said, loading the few remaining rounds and clamping the chamber shut. A twitch of pain reminded him to take it slow, but now, slow meant death, therefore he pushed both aside. His eyes fell on the giant boom arm which extended up and out over the entire garage. The conveyor boom was used to dump harvested corn onto a nearby truck that followed behind it.

This guy enjoys the sound of his voice. Let's use it. "Is this your way of calling it quits?" Antonio asked, while he climbed the small ladder on the harvester's side.

Swinging out from cover with his weapon up and pressed tight to his shoulder, Lester crept towards the opposite end of the garage, one step placed carefully in front of the other, closing in on his target.

"Well, my mom simply called it southern hospitality," Lester responded, swiftly snapping the gun between each aisle, but seeing nothing.

All was quiet as he approached the last vehicle in line, the John Deere harvester. With his back against the front of the vehicle, he spun with his gun up and latched on the trigger, releasing a loud barrage of gunfire, which soared toward where he thought his target was hiding. A second later, he looked around for a body, but realized he had only killed air. He felt the finger of panic crawling up his back. He took a deep breath, glancing around for movement, trying not to panic, but sweat began to bead on his forehead. *How can I be sweating when it's so fricking cold out here,* he thought.

"Nice trick there," Lester said, spinning to cover all directions, as he spoke. "Where you go, buddy?" He continued this motion, when he saw a shadow engulfing his peripheral vision from above. He raised his barrel to fire, but Antonio had beat him to the punch.

Jumping from the boom, Antonio fired his remaining shots. The gunfire whizzed through the air. The first two missed completely, but the last one struck true, hitting Lester in the shoulder that was bracing the MP5.

"AHHHHH!" He screamed, as he felt the bullet penetrate his flesh; the searing, throbbing pain followed. "AHHHHH!" he hollered loudly. The round went clean through flesh and bone, exiting out his rear shoulder blade. The blast lurching him backward, as he grasped his shoulder, trying to maintain his balance. Dazed and in shock, he failed to recover.

Antonio hurled him to the ground, knocking the weapon from Lester's hand, sending it sliding from view. Both men rolled away from each other and stumbled to their feet. Now standing face to face, they instinctively took to their fighting stance, their eyes locked in a death stare, as they slowly circled the other.

"You'll be my appetizer, 'cause I'm gonna kill you first. The old man will be my main course. Then, I'll have a bit of fun with your girlfriend before I finish her for my dessert," Lester whispered with a sneer, his voice harsh and cold. He followed with a jab, which Antonio easily sidestepped.

"You seem a little slow on the uptake for a merc," Antonio grunted, throwing a straight punch of his own, which Lester side-stepped.

"I told you I was warming up," Lester growled, parrying the attack.

Antonio quickly followed up with several jabs. All the blows were blocked or evaded, except for the last one, which Antonio fake jabbed with the left, only to throw a crossover with his right. The attack nicked Lester's chin and slammed heavily into his wounded shoulder.

Stumbling backward, grunting with pain, Lester quickly regained his balance, took a deep breath, and squared off. "Have to give it to you, you're some pilot," he said, glaring at Antonio's now bloody knuckles. "But I'm warm now!"

As the words left Lester's lips, he moved rapidly in full motion with a front jab that Antonio swiped down. He followed with a hard punch and kick, which took Antonio by surprise, as it slammed into his chest, sending him crashing into the harvester's large wheel. Antonio grunted, as he felt something pop, and the pain intensified and radiated through his body, as he slid down the wheel to his knees.

"I said you're good, but you're not me," Lester smiled. "Yeah, I saw you favoring your ribs when you came out of the house. Never, ever show your weakness." A stiff jab to the jaw sent Antonio to the floor. "Whoa!" Lester shouted, shaking his extremities, then rolled Antonio over onto his back. "I'm going to savor this moment by killing you the old-fashioned way, boy. The rush always gets me," he muttered, kneeling to wrap his hands around Antonio's throat.

Antonio scooted away on his back, trying to escape the hold, but his attacker held on tight to him, following his every move.

"There's no escaping this," Lester grinned, bearing his weight down on Antonio's neck.

Antonio began coughing up blood and saliva with each gasp of breath. With little to no options remaining, he used what strength he had left to try and twist away to loosen the grip on his neck, but with his ribs now broken on one side, he couldn't move his body the way he wanted.

Lester saw what Antonio was trying to do. He laughed as he rendered a prompt knee to the groin, slightly ended Antonio's effort.

"It'll be over soon," Lester leaned in and whispered into his ear, saliva cascading from his lips onto Antonio's face. His prey's struggling pulse and breaths only excited him further, as he took pleasure staring down into Antonio's fleeting eyes.

Antonio felt helpless. He was too weak to struggle anymore, and his breathing was labored. *Is this it? Is this how I'm going to die, on some farm in the middle of nowhere.* He thought. *I wish I could have gotten my life straight before taking this one-way trip outta here.* Just when Antonio's last breath was near, a loud shot rang out and blood splattered across his face. Antonio looked up, and a hole emerged in Lester's chest, where his heart should have been. The body went limp and slumped, falling on top of him. Still struggling for air, Antonio shoved the dead weight off him, and quickly massaged his throat, trying to suck in more air.

Lana looked shocked at what she had just done. Dropping Betsy in horror, she ran to Antonio, scooping him up in her arms. "Oh my, God, oh my, God!" Are you okay?" she asked frantically.

"He broke my ribs. I can't breathe," Antonio whispered with a raspy voice, as he attempted to sit up.

"Don't move, sounds like one of your lungs might be compromised," Lana said, her hands and eyes going up and down, examining his body.

As shock settled in, he grabbed her hand.

"Hey, hey, stay with me," Lana said, his eyes gazing past her.

Antonio shuddered at the cold which was enveloping his whole body.

"You can't give up now. Not now! Gabby! Daddy! I need you, now!" Lana cried, tears welling in her eyes.

Antonio's world began to fade to black. And for a moment, he felt nothing as he took in Lana's face for what he thought would be the last time, the snow slowly descending behind her. There was no pain, no struggle.

"I'm glad, we—"

Then, there was nothing.

Epilogue

Three days have passed since the storm ended and Antonio was arrested. It had been a very difficult time for the Morris family as they tried coping with all that had transpired. While John spent the last few days in the hospital for emergency surgery to repair the tendon in his knee, Lana and Gabby returned to the cabin to board up broken windows and patch bullet holes. The family had come to the agreement it was best to wait until the warm season to do any other major repairs. The most important thing for them was to try to rest and relax, which they had initially planned to do during their vacation. Lana had been struggling with nightmares ever since the shootout and how it ended. She was glad that Gabby hadn't seen any of it.

"Gabby, don't forget to grab Pop's luggage. It's at the foot of his bed," Lana yelled as she stopped near the steps when she heard the local news on the living room television.

"In other news, the FBI has been called in to assist with the Warroad National Bank robbery when the case went cold after local authorities found the robbers' burnt vehicle behind Warroad High School," the brunette news anchor announced. "The thirty-three-year-old former Army helicopter pilot, Antonio Hampton, who was allegedly involved in the robbery, remains in custody. His two accomplices, who have recently been identified as thirty-eight-year-old Lester Dash and millionaire Ramsey Pacey's twenty-nine-year-old son, Brad Pacey. Lester Dash was found dead when authorities arrived at the scene of a shootout at a local family's cabin just off North Route 313. Brad Pacey was found dead inside a helicopter crash in the woods a few miles from the family cabin. The FBI has yet to reveal more information regarding the bank robbery, those involved, or what went wrong. However, leading sources suggest the bank was targeted by Brad Pacey as large sums of money had been transferred into the bank only days before. Those funds were going to be used to help fund Warroad's new public works initiative. The funds were provided by business tycoon, Ramsey Pacey, who has yet to comment on his son's involvement. The funds have been recovered."

"Lana, have you seen my charger anywhere?" Gabby asked from upstairs, breaking Lana's trance from the television.

"Yeah, yeah." attempting to gather herself, "It's down here on the kitchen counter where you left it."

Giving the news a final look, her heart sank, as she continued to walk toward the door, where she was immediately bathed in the sunlight of a clear sky. For a moment, she stood still at the top of the front steps and allowed the sun's rays to warm her, thinking that somehow they could brighten her day and erase the madness. The last few days seemed like a lifetime. With luggage in tow, she proceeded down the stairs towards their vehicle.

Their 2012 Honda Pilot trunk door had been open for the last thirty minutes as they loaded up their belongings from the trip. Tossing in one of her bags, she inhaled deep breaths and reflected on all that happened with Gabby, Pops, and her coming to the cabin to rekindle their family spirit. It was more than she bargained for, from her and her dad arguing as they both dealt with past hurts, to the crazy shootout. Yet, through it all, her mind kept going back to the stranger who had knocked on their door to get out of the storm.

She had only known Antonio for three days, and now she could not get him out of her head. *What does it matter? Yes, he did assist in a crime, but he also helped to save me and my family*, she thought as she tossed in the last bag.

Lana began to feel something she had not felt in years. But the hardest part about it all was she never had the opportunity to say thank you. Her eyes and shoulders became heavy as tears began to well up, sobbing, she failed to sense the figure approaching from behind.

"Leaving already?" someone asked.

Straightening up, she slowly turned to face the familiar voice.

About the Authors

Tiffany Gibbs, who also writes under the pen name Tiffany Michele, is an author who crosses genres. Whether it is nonfiction, science fiction, or poetry, Tiffany enjoys it all. She enjoys writing books for children, as well as for young adults, and adult readers. Tiffany's love of reading started early and grew as she began to craft her own stories from an early age. She aims to encourage, inspire, and educate in her stories. Based out of Baltimore, Tiffany is originally from Virginia Beach, VA.

Dameon Gibbs holds a Bachelor of Art in Anthropology and World History and an Master of Art in Classical Studies. For the past five years, he has worked with inner-city youth in Baltimore, Maryland. He has been an avid writer since his days in high school during the late 1990s. He enjoys the creative process of all writing genres, whether it be religious, poetic, science fiction, historical, biographies, or action adventure. Dameon is married to fellow author Tiffany Michele.